Anonymous

The adopted daughter

The trials of Sabra : A tale of real life

Anonymous

The adopted daughter
The trials of Sabra : A tale of real life

ISBN/EAN: 9783337137533

Printed in Europe, USA, Canada, Australia, Japan

Cover: Foto ©Andreas Hilbeck / pixelio.de

More available books at **www.hansebooks.com**

THE

ADOPTED DAUGHTER;

OR, THE

TRIALS OF SABRA.

A TALE OF REAL LIFE.

Fourth Edition—Revised and Amended.

Montreal:

JOHN LOVELL, PRINTER, ST. NICHOLAS STREET.

1873.

PREFACE

TO THE FOURTH EDITION.

THE following Narrative is one of real life. The object of the Authoress in presenting it to the public is to encourage those to persevere who are left to depend upon their own exertions. She has endeavored to present it in language that will have a moral and religious influence upon the minds of those who may peruse it.

This is the sincere wish of

THE WRITER,

CHAPTER I.

MR. AND MRS. HUDSON.

Samuel Hudson was the son of a farmer, in good circumstances, who lived in the town of S., M. county, Massachusetts; and in the town of C., near by, lived Miss Ordelia Wilder, his affianced bride. She was the daughter of a farmer, who died, leaving his widow with nine children, some of them quite small. They were all industrious, and having one of the best of mothers to superintend the management of their affairs, they succeeded in keeping their farm, and acquired a good living. They were brought up in a strict observance of good, moral, and religious principles.

Samuel and Ordelia were married at an early age. They selected a farm, for their future residence, upon the lovely banks of the Nashua river, in the county of W., where they lived for many years, happily and contentedly. They gradually increased in wealth, and often enlargened the borders of their farm. In a few years they became wealthy and independent. It is true, they labored hard, but what of that, when they could see the fruit of it.

Within five years after their marriage, they were blessed with three lovely sons. The eldest was named Jason, after his grandfather H.; the second, Frederick, after his grandfather W., and the youngest, Samuel, and for a long time the fond mother called him her babe. Ordelia did not choose to keep any servants, consequently she had to work very hard. Their farm, at that time, was not all paid for, and she did not think they were able to hire. There was only sixteen months' difference in the ages of Jason and Fred; and often did Ordelia spin her day's work, with Fred in her apron: he was always peevish, and would never be quiet away from his mother. Often would she milk four or five cows, with him on her lap, and Jason beside her. Hard, indeed, did this dear mother labor to accumulate property, which, in the decline of life, she had not the liberty of controlling. Alas! how little do some children realize, when they become men and women, how much trouble, anxiety, and care they have caused their parents in their childhood. They seem to think their parents must conform entirely to their wishes. Far better would it be for them, if they indulge them with that kindness with which they were indulged in their childhood. Jason was a noble, generous hearted boy, too liberal for his own good; he loved everybody, and everybody loved him. He was always kind to his parents: their slightest wish was his will, and he always performed it with pleasure. Frederick's character did not develop as much in manhood. He was one of the still ones, rather selfish ; but on the whole might be called an obedient child.   Samuel was different from either ; he had a mind of his own ; he was not disobedient, but would generally have his own way, either by argument or by teasing, and he would also tease for his brothers, as well as for himself.   Consequently he was sometimes called " the tease."   They were all very industrious, and their father thought this was of more consequence than acquiring an education.   He was willing they should have the advantage of a country district school, and this was all he thought necessary ; this was all the privilege he had received, and it would do very well for them ; but Samuel managed, somehow, to obtain an education superior to the rest.   He afterwards became competent to teach a village school.

CHAPTER II.

THEIR DAUGHTER.

Ordelia toiled excessively, with her household duties, not thinking that her unceasing labours were gradually breaking down her strong constitution, and that eventually she would suffer the consequence of so doing. Alas ! as the worm commences at the root of the plant, and in an invisible manner hinders the progress of its

growth, so, also, Ordelia was slowly destroying her
health.   The day arrived when they expected another
to bless their family circle.   Great hopes were entertained that the little stranger might be a daughter ; to
their joy their hopes were realized.   Alas! how often
when the heart rejoices in the very height of happiness,
the cherished blessing is removed, and that heart is
left to bleed with anguish, untill it saps at the fountain
springs of life.   So it was with them.

The fair flower was taken away, e'er she knew her
mother's smiles.   Many think that the death of an
infant, before it has entwined itself around the affections,
by its tender smiles, and its winning voice, is but a
small source of sorrow.   'Tis not so with the fond
mother, who in her anguish has seen her beloved infant
form carried away, and she unable to follow to see
where they have laid it.   How sadly does she feel
the loss.   She even longs to bestow that care upon
some object, which it would have been her pleasure to
have performed for her child.   She arouses from her
quiet slumber at the slightest noise.   It is my child,
is the first thought flits through her mind.   But, alas !
she finds her child is not there, and the encouraging
truth flashes across her aching breast, that she will
never more behold its lovely face in this world ; that
it is among the bright angels of God, who are his peculiar favourites ; and perhaps, at that very moment, its
little spirit is hovering around her head, whispering
this cheering sentence, " Weep not for me. "

Deeply, very deeply, did Ordelia feel the loss of her little infant, and slowly did she regain her health. When she recovered, her anxiety increased to be without servants. As soon as possible, she dismissed them, and attended to her domestic duties herself. Her manifold cares seemed to divert her mind from her loss, but there was still a vacuum in her heart, which the other children could not fill. They were out at work with their father during the day; indeed they were not as fond of being petted as many children, but were aspiring to see which could be the most like a man ; which could do the most work ; or which could shoot at target the best, which was a favorite amusement for them all.

CHAPTER III.

THE INTRODUCTION TO SABRA.

One morning Mr. Hudson came in from his field, and requested his wife to mix for him a mug of molasses, ginger, and water. Ordelia was nursing Sabra. She had been straightening her flaxen hair, and making little curls. She was a beautiful little child, one year old ; her eyes sparkled with brightness ; they were of that expression which speaks the sentiments of the heart plainer than language. She placed the child upon the floor, and she cast back upon her a grateful look, which fully recompensed Ordelia for all her trouble. Mr. Hudson commenced playing with her; she attempted to climb upon his knee; he took her up, and was caressing her as Ordelia entered, with the ginger and water prepared. He took a draught, and then asked Ordelia what she intended to do with Sabra? Ordelia looked at her husband, with one of those tender glances, which an affectionate, loving wife bestows upon her companion, when about to ask a favor, and then replied, " I intend to keep her, if you are willing. Her mother says she will give her to us, if we will adopt her, and bring her up as one of ours; you know that she loves me already as dearly as if I were her mother. She has been with us but a few weeks, and she has already won our affections. " Samuel looked very thoughtful. He soon replied: " I have no objections; if you choose to keep her, I am perfectly willing if we can have the whole control of her; but I should not wish to have her mother see her often, lest it should make her discontented."

" You need not fear that, " said Ordelia, " for her mother is going to leave this, and is anxious to have us take her; says she will not come here except to enquire after her health. She says, we can bring her up and give her a better education than she can, and she will leave her entirely to us, if we will adopt her; and I wish to, if I keep her. It seems to me, that she would repair the loss of our little daughter. She is very winning in her nature, and tiny ways; I love her dearly, and feel as if I could not part with her ;" and she pressed the child tenderly to her boson, saying : " No, my darling, I cannot part with you. I think the boys will love her too. Jason is fond of her already, and often brings her playthings ; but you know that the other boys never notice children : they may love her, after a while cannot avoid it, for every body seems to love her." " And she is to call us papa and mamma ?" said Samuel. " Certainly," said Ordelia, " she calls me mamma already." " Well," said Samuel, " I think it a very good plan ; " and it was fully decided that they would adopt Sabra as their daughter. Her mother was informed of their decision, and consented to their requirements.

CHAPTER IV.

SABRA'S CHILDHOOD.

Her days of childhood were indeed happy days. She knew nothing of want. She was, naturally, cheerful and happy, and never had trouble, as many other children, but was happy in the thought of loving and being loved. When the boys were informed by their parents that they had adopted Sabra as their daughter, Fred or Samuel did not seem to care about it, either way, but Jason was well pleased ; he said, she would be company for his mother, and soon be able to help her. He said she was no trouble to any person.

He soon won her affections by his kindness, and he always loved her as a sister. She, unconscious little creature, knew no difference. She would climb upon her father's knee, whenever he came in, and he was always ready to receive her. Jason made a nice little trundle-bed for her, and took her to the shop, and placed her in it, and drew her to the house. He often made playthings for her amusement. All these kindnesses were treasured up in her little memory, never to be forgotten. Sabra had been sick for a few days, was recovering, but had no appetite; Jason was sitting with her upon the door step; there came a squirrel running past; Jason picked up a stone, threw it, and killed the squirrel. He dressed it, and said Sabra could eat it: his mother cooked it. She ate that, and it seemed to increase her appetite. Afterwards, he killed wild game for her, every day, until she was quite well.

CHAPTER V.

JASON'S SICKNESS.

The three sons worked very hard: Jason, being the eldest, took the heaviest part of the work. This proved a great injury to him, for he worked and lifted more than he was able to bear. He wrenched his side, which brought on a severe sickness, and was never healthy afterwards. For a long time they did not expect him to recover ; and when he began to amend, it was slowly, for his constitution was impaired ; and it was decided that he was not able, or strong enough, to work on the farm.

———

CHAPTER VI.

THE NEW HOUSE.

The house that stood upon the farm which they bought was getting very old, and began to decay. It was also too small for their family. Samuel had been making preparations to build for a long time. He was one of those close, calculating men, who was always using economy to save money ; and all that could be done by themselves, was thought of and contrived to the best advantage. He thought he would build of brick, for he could have them made upon his own farm, and that would save expense ; he was calculating to build a large house, and have it finished neatly.

He was able to have it built exactly to his mind, and he expected it to cost him, at at least, three thousand dollars. He had his men employed ; and at the commencement, he said to Ordelia, he was afraid that Sabra would be in the way, while they had such a large family, or that she would get hurt among the timber, or sharp-edged tools. Ordelia had feared the

same, and had been talking with Mrs. Heulet, their
nearest neighbour, about it.   Mrs. Heulet had very
kindly offered to have Sabra come and stay with them
while they were building.   Ordelia told her husband,
and he thought she had better consent to let her go
for a short time.   She very reluctantly consented.
Every night, after her work was done, she would go
and see her, and tell her that, in a few days, she should
come back, and have a nice large house to live in, and
have a nice closet for her clothes, and a shelf in it for
her doll; but it so happened, that she did not stay long,
for one day, as she was playing, she accidentally fell
partly in some hot water, that was left standing on the
floor and was badly scalded.   Ordelia's troubles were
now increased, for she could not feel easy about her,
although she well knew all was done for her that
could be desired.   One evening, she asked Sabra if
she wished to go home with mamma.   She quickly
replied that she did, and that Jason could take care of
her; that she should soon be well, if she could be at
home.   Her mother took her in her arms, and carried
her home, and with careful nursing she soon recovered.
Mrs. Heulet was very kind to Sabra, and allowed her
to call her aunt.   She had a son, who had been married a short time previous, living in the same family.
They were also very fond of Sabra, and she served as
a plaything, and became much attached to them, and
has ever since remained so.   We shall have occasion
to speak of their kindness hereafter.

One morning, Katy, the hired girl, came running into the house, and said to Mrs. Hudson, "Come and see Jason!" She went to the door, and was quite frightened, for Jason had Sabra nearly to the top of the ladder, and was taking her to the roof of the building, where the men were shingling the house. It was very large ; two stories high. He kept her there some time, for it pleased her exceedingly to gaze off upon the large green flats. She has related to me how beautifully everything looked while she stood upon the top of that house. Jason took her down safely, and led her to her mother, and told her she need not fear that he would let her fall, for he was always careful of her. Sabra was playing with the blocks, and the master builder said to her : "You are a very little girl, to be trudging about here." "Yes, sir," she replied, " I am little but good." She was always ready to give them an answer, which often amused them very much. They were all very kind to her ; and this was a great comfort to her mother, for she loved her dearly, and was very indulgent to her, and allowed her to play out around the door ; and by so doing, she found her but very little trouble.

CHAPTER VII.

THE FIRST PUNISHMENT.

After the house was completed, and the family had removed into it, Mrs. Hudson was turning a large cheese,

B

to put back into the press, for they had a large dairy. She was paring off the tender rind and giving it to Sabra, who was very fond of it, and was always watching to get it. Mrs. Hudson had left a large cheese upon the table, without trimming it : Sabra thought she would help herself ; she commenced nibbling off the rind, and nearly spoiled the cheese. When her mother saw the mischief done to the cheese, she was not sure which had broken it ; she was confident it was either Sabra or the cat. She called Sabra, and asked her if she had eaten the cheese ; she replied, " Yes, mamma." " You little rogue, you, your mamma will punish you, if you spoil another cheese." Sabra looked as if astonished to hear of punishment. She did not cry ; she seldom had any trouble to cause her to shed tears ; but went to play as if nothing had happened. A few days after this Mrs. Hudson left another cheese in the same manner. Sabra was playing about as usual, and, seeing it, she began to break off the rind, as she previously had done ; and ate all she wished for, without thinking of her mamma's commands. Mrs. Hudson soon saw what had befallen the cheese ; she called Sabra, and asked her if she had broken it. She promptly replied, " Yes, mamma." " But do you not recollect I told you I should punish you if you spoiled another cheese ? Which is your choice, to be whipped, or be shut in the cellar ?" Sabra quickly replied : " I had rather be whipped." " Then I shall put you in the cellar." She took her by the hand, and led her down the stairs, and placed her in one of the arches which formed a closet, and closed the door. She went to the top of the stairs, and stopped to listen, for she expected she would be frightened; but, to her surprise, she did not say a word for some minutes. She then called her mamma, and asked how long she had to stay there. Her mamma did not answer her, but waited, expecting to hear her cry.

After some minutes, she commenced crying, and her mother hastened to let her out of her prison. She never again nibbled a cheese. Her mother has often said, that she never, after this, had cause to punish her for disobedience. She would also say, " Very few mothers have as little trouble with their children as I have with Sabra."

CHAPTER VIII.

THE PARTING WITH JASON.

It was finally decided that Jason should go to a trade. This was a great affliction to his mother and Sabra. He was not as healthy as the other boys, and his mother felt quite anxious about him ; he was exceedingly kind to her, and also to Sabra, who loved him dearly, and delighted to be with him. If he went to walk he would let her go ; if he went to catch pigeons with a net, he would let her lay the bait ; if he was from home, she would watch for his return. After

he left home she was very lonely; if he was expected,
she would seat herself at the door, or window, and look
for him ; if told that she must go to bed, she would lie
awake and listen, to hear his voice.   He would always
go and speak to her ; and, if allowed, she would get up.
He always brought something to please her.   If asked
who she loved the best, she would say, " mamma, and
papa, and Jason."

Sabra often wondered why Frederick and Samuel
did not love her as Jason did.   Sometimes she would
fancy that Samuel did love her, for he often called upon
her to wait on him, to bring his boots, his hat or his coat,
and as she became older, she would take care of them ;
sometimes put strings in his shoes, brush his coat, and
hang it up.   He was kind to her, but she loved and
feared him, for he would always reprove her, if he
thought she had done wrong.   Sometimes she would
grieve and shed tears alone.   When about six years
old, she had the whooping-cough, and was coughing
very severely on the door step : she heard Samuel say
to his mother that he did not believe she had the
whooping-cough, but he thought she made it.   Now,
Sabra was very conscientious, and very sensitive : it
grieved her exceedingly ; her mother found her crying,
as if her heart would break; she soon cheered and
soothed her sorrows by her kindness.   Often was
her feeling heart almost broken by such remarks,
while she was ignorant of the true cause.

One day there came a lady there : Sabra did not

like her, she thought she appeared strange; she
thought her mother was not very glad to see her, she
knew not why; but she did not stay long : Sabra was
glad, for she thought her mother was afraid to have
her talk with her. After she was gone, Fred told
Sabra, that woman was her other mamma, and that
some day she would come and take her away. Sabra
did not believe him ; she soon went to her mamma, and
told her what Fred had said. Her mother said " Poh !
it is all nonsense ; Fred only said that to tease you :
there will no person carry away my darling child ; I
could not spare you." Sabra learned to make herself
useful, when quite young; she would gather chips,
bring wood, and thus save her mamma many steps.
She learned different kinds of employment ; when only
five years old, she knit herself a pair of stockings, and
then began to knit for the family. She would knit
the foot of a man's sock in a day, easily, and performed
her task with pleasure, for she took delight in being
praised.

CHAPTER IX.

SABRA'S SCHOOL DAYS.

Sabra's advantages for acquiring an education
were limited. Living in the country, and the district
being small, they employed a teacher only a few
weeks during the year ; generally ten or twelve weeks

in the winter, and seven weeks in the summer; and
in the latter, the girls devoted much of their time to
needle work, their mothers thinking it more profitable
for them to learn there, than for them to spend their
time to learn them at home.

Very few books were used in the common schools,
and at the end of each term, they must be carefully
laid aside, in some box or drawer, and remain there
until the commencement of another term. Few books
were accessible in that family. The Bible, the Hymn
Book, and Bunyan's Pilgrim's Progress, with three or
four other books, were thought quite sufficient. The
knitting work was a far more important occupation
for the leisure moments. Sabra was confined to the
common spelling book in school, until she had nearly
committed it to memory. By hearing the older scholars recite grammer, she had nearly committed that
to memory also. One day her teacher told her she
might study grammar, if she would bring one to school.
She was very much pleased, and hastened to tell her
mamma. Her mother was willing, and said, perhaps
Samuel would let her have his old one. Samuel was
willing, and gave her that, and an old English Reader ;
and Fred gave her an Arithmetic ; with those books,
she felt quite pleased. Her teacher was surprised to
see with what ease she committed her lessons. The
first time her brother Jason came home, she asked him
to give her his old Geography and Atlas : he cheerfully
gave them to her. Some of the maps were nearly

worn out, but she managed to change with Henrietta Heulet, her class-mate, and by so doing, she always had her lessons perfectly. Henrietta and Sabra were great friends, and were always striving to see which could be at the head of the class. At one time, the inspector, Mr. Allen, said to the committee, that Henrietta and Sabra might be weighed in almost any balance and not be found wanting. This encouraged them to persevere, and they were remarkable scholars, considering the limited privileges they enjoyed.

CHAPTER X.

THE SUBJECT OF RELIGION.

Sabra became the subject of religious impressions at an early age. When only ten years old, she would retire alone, and pray God to forgive her sins and change her heart. She was a Sabbath-school scholar, when Sabbath-schools were first organized in that section ; and continued connected with it for many years, and became a teacher. When she was about ten years old, there was a revival of religion in the church where she attended worship. Her mother, for many years, had been thought to be a Christian, and was exemplary for piety, and early instructed Sabra in the path of virtue and religion. At one time, previous to this revival, she placed her hand upon Sabra's head, and earnestly and fervently prayed to God to convert her child, and make her an heir of glory. This one prayer, Sabra never forgot. Still, Mrs. Hudson had no abiding evidence in her own heart of her acceptance with God, but, like Thomas, filled with doubts and fears, she was waiting for some wonderful manifestation of Divine power. It was not so with her father, or the boys. They were worldly-minded, and sought for their pleasure in worldly amusements. Upright in their dealings, they thought this sufficient. But, at the time of this reformation, Mr. Hudson became serious, and gave the subject of religion his attention, and was hopefully converted to God, and became a useful member in the church. During the revival, and just as light began to dawn upon Mrs. Hudson's mind, there was a great excitement, caused by a remark made by Mr. W., a member of the church, who, it was always thought, possessed more religion in the head than heart. Mr. and Mrs. Hudson, and Sabra, were at the meeting, and at the close, Mr. W. came and said to Mrs. Hudson, " I have lately been spoken to by the Lord concerning you ; unless you turn to God immediately, go forward and make a public confession of religion, you will be left in the greatest horror of mind that ever any poor creature experienced ; darkness and despair will come upon you, and you will be left without hope." This alarmed her very much ; and she, being of a nervous temperament, and not enjoying good health at the time, went home almost in despair. And, truly, deep darkness overclouded her mind. While she saw her companion, and others, rejoicing in the first fruits of pardoning love, she was overwhelmed in darkness: the state of her mind impaired her bodily health, and she became unable to attend to her household duties, and soon was confined to her room. It then became necessary for them to employ a housekeeper. They employed a girl named Betsy; some called her an old maid; but she was a member of the church, consequently she must be considered suitable. She, too, had more religion in the head, than heart; her tongue was never tired either talking to Mr. H. or singing; she would often induce him to sing with her, and make the house ring. This was no comfort to Mrs. H., in her trying situation of body and mind; besides this, Betsey did not seem to like Sabra, but seemed to watch her with a jealous eye, and often found fault with her without just cause. Sabra's mother felt very tender towards her and liked to have her present with her most of the time. Sabra would sit by her bedside, and give her medicine when necessary. She often read of chapters comfort and consolation from the Bible. Her mother would request her often to read the eighty-eighth Psalm; she thought it applicable to herself. Many of the Psalms of David, and the afflictions of Job, seemed to bring comfort to her mind.

She did not expect to recover her health, and her greatest worldly trouble was for Sabra's welfare. She would say : " What will become of Sabra when I am gone ?" Mr. Hudson assured her, that Sabra should be well provided for; and often promised her, in the presence of Sabra, and others, that his property should be equally divided among the four children, when he had done with it, and he would not neglect to attend to it during his lifetime.

Jason had left home; he was more delicate than the other boys, and needed more assistance; this caused his mother many an anxious thought. Her husband assured her, that she need have no trouble on their account, for Jason and Sabra should share equally with the others.

All Sabra desired was her mother's recovery. Young as she was, she often prayed earnestly for this. She seemed to understand her mother's trials, and to sympathize with her, and often endeavored to cheer her heart by quoting passages from the Scriptures. She felt assured that her mother was a Christian, and labored to persuade her to think the same of herself. Mrs. Hudson believed, that the sacrament of the Lord's Supper was prepared for every name or denomination; and being filled with doubts and fears in regard to her own acceptance with Christ, she could not see it her duty to partake of this ordniance with her husband.

The winter season, with its dreary aspect and its chilling effect upon the gloomy mind, gradually passed away, and spring, sweet spring with its balmy influence, ushered in to cheer the despondent heart, and Mrs. Hudson's bodily health began to improve. She was soon able to walk out, and view the wonderful works of nature, the handy-work of that God, whom she had been wont to adore and worship, with love and reverence. Sometimes she would think, if she had never been converted she would not be subject to such feelings, and she occasionally had a faint hope ; her spirits gradually revived ; and, during the summer, she was able, with Sabra's assistance, to attend to her household duties and to dismiss Betsey : this was a great relief to them both, for neither of them liked her. Sabra's religious impressions never left her; she viewed the Saviour as the giver of all her blessings, and always thought it her duty to pray to him as her benefactor ; still, she had not the hope of a Christian, until past her eighteenth year. She always took great delight in the Sabbath-school, and was seldom absent from church. Their parson, the Rev. Mr. Saunderson, had six sons: the two eldest were twins ; they were a year older than Sabra ; she had been accustomed to see them at church, from her earliest recollection ; they always recited a large number of verses. Sabra watched them with a critical eye, and strove to recite as many verses as they did; she was unwilling to have them excel her in anything. She thought them the best boys in school ; and the fact was, she thought their equal could not be found. These were her early impressions ; but more on this subject hereafter.

Often, while reciting from the Holy Scriptures, and while listening to remarks in the Sabbath school, would Sabra resolve to give her heart to Christ and become a Christian; she seemed to have clear views of what was requisite, but being of a lively temperament, and somewhat gay, the cares and pleasures of the world overcame her resolutions, and she remained the same, always convicted of sin and of duty, but unconverted. Her mother was less anxious about her literary attainments than her domestic improvements. She was anxious to give her a knowledge of all kinds of domestic employment. Sabra learned to make butter and cheese, to spin and weave, to braid straw, to work lace, and to turn her hand to any employment, whereby she might earn a shilling. With the proceeds, she purchased her clothing. She thus learned, while very young, to depend upon her own industry, which was great benefit to her in after years. Between the age of twelve and fifteen many memorable events transpired, which are recorded in the following chapter.

CHAPTER XI.

THE TWO MARRIAGES.

Frederick always lived at home, and was called bashful, but he married first. It did not require much courage to win his bride, for he married his cousin, Marina Bronson. She was possessed of some good qualities, and became an amiable woman. But, at this time, she possessed a large phrenological development upon the top of her head, which made her aware of all her good qualities. She could braid more yards of straw in a day than any one else ; she could make a cheese in the morning, and cut and make a pair of pants in the same day; she could wash and iron, and go to the neighbours and tell it ; could spin two days work in one. These were valuable qualities in a family like this, for there was plenty to be done. She was gay, dressy, and proud, and always thought her own way the best.

Mrs. Hudson being of a yielding disposition, Marina soon found it an easy matter to rule in most things. It soon became evident that she did not like Sabra, and her remarks often caused Mrs. Hud on much grief. Sabra tried very hard to please her, but she often had cause to weep, in consequence of Marina's taunting remarks. Their mother was a real peace-maker, and told Sabra that she must not notice them ; but be a good girl, and all would be right by and by.

Sabra had always worked very hard, and had had the promise of many privileges, when the boys got married. One was, she should go to school ; but she saw no prospect of doing so, for worldly-mindedness seemed to increase, and to know how to do all kinds of work seemed to be the main object. Sabra and her mother could see that Fred's mind was becoming prejudiced, for formerly he had never spoken harshly to Sabra, but was indifferent ; now he often found fault with her. This grieved her often, but she knew the cause, and feared the result.

Fred and his wife lived by themselves, and had half of
the house, it being large enough for two families. Samuel
had been from home much of the time for three or
four years ; he did not like to work on the farm. He
was soon to be married ; and his father thought he had
better bring his wife home, for the farm was large
enough for all ; they could live with him in the family,
until they could build, and then he would take the
new house, and the boys (as he called them) could
have the large one. Samuel married a farmer's
daughter, in the same town ; she was different from
Fred's wife, in almost every respect. The peacock
and the dove might compare as well as these two
persons. Asenath, Samuel's wife, was equally as
smart for business, and could do as much as Marina,
but she had not the faculty of telling of it. She was
unassuming in every respect, and mild and for-
bearing ; she thought others as good, or better than
herself; kind to all, and especially to Sabra ; and Sabra
loved her dearly; she thought her a very dear sister.
She knew very well that Asenath loved her as a sister,
and treated her as such ; she was always happy while
with her : and it was always a p'easure for her to do
her, or Samuel, a favor. Samuel was quite willing
to be waited upon, and always called upon Sabra.

Jason lived in the town of C., about eighteen miles
distant. News came that he would bring his intended
bride to his father's, on a visit. Great preparations
were made for their entertainment ; for report said she

was quite a lady, and a school teacher. Sabra was very careful to have everything in its proper place, and to be as tidy as possible. She longed to see Jason, but feared that she would not dare to speak to the lady. She felt sure that if Jason liked her, she would like her too. But, oh! if she should meet her displeasure, would she not influence Jason to dislike her; this thought she could not bear, and she gave vent to her grief by a flood of tears. Thus soliloquised Sabra, the day before their arrival. She knew there would be much work to be performed, for they kept no servants, as they do now, and she intended to do all she could, that her mother might sit down, and visit, with her.

It was a beautiful summer's day; the sun beamed calmly upon the fields and upon the towering oaks; it was shady at the front of the house, and all were ready for their reception. Sabra had been watching for them, from the chamber window; she had seen a chaise in the distance, and she thought it must be them; she went down stairs and told her mother they were coming. Mrs. Hudson took her spectacles off and quietly folded them together, and laid them by and waited their arrival. Marina was all on tiptoe, as usual, as if she was all the person to be seen. Not so with the quiet Asenath; she kept back and let her mother have an introduction first. After all had an introduction, Jason came to Sabra, and appeared very glad to see her. Henrietta, for this was the lady's name, followed, and clasping Sabra's hand, said: " And this is your little

sister, I have so often heard you speak of ? " How those
words thrilled through Sabra's heart ; her embarrass-
ment was all gone, and she thought she never heard a
voice so sweet, or saw a form so graceful ; if she was
a lady, she thought she would like very much to be one
herself.   When they went to milk, Henrietta went trip-
ping along with them. She had always lived in a village,
and had never milked a cow.   She thought it very
strange that Sabra could milk, she was so small.
Marina tried very hard to engross all her attention, by
talking as fast as possible, but Henrietta would listen
to others as well as her, and would often talk with
Sabra.

The next day, in the morning, the boys went out to
hunt for wild game.   After dinner, they talked of
taking a pleasure ride ; they were going to the adjoining town. Sabra was not accustomed to hear of pleasure
riding ; she thought it would be very nice, three bellows-
topped chaises in a row.   She expected to stay at
home, but Jason said that Sabra might go with them.
" Yes," said Henrietta, " come my dear girl, and get
ready."   Asenath said she would assist her in getting
ready ; her father and mother were very glad to have
her go.   She was nearly ready, when Fred came in.
He inquired where she was going ? His mother said,
" She is going with Jason."   " Oh, pshaw ! " said
Fred, " we don't want her ; " and Marina said she
" should not think she would want to go ; but it was just
like her ; " and she flirted out of the room muttering to

herself. Asenath said she saw no reason why Sabra should stay at home; she would like to have her go. But Samuel, seeing how opposed Fred and Marina were, said she had better stay at home. Everything must be as he said; and Sabra took off her bonnet. Her little heart was near bursting with grief, but she said not a word. Henrietta said: " Do not feel disappointed, I will give you this," taking a beautiful necklace from her own neck, and placing it upon Sabra's, who thought she had never seen anything as beautiful. She had often thought she would like to ask Henrietta to let her see it, but she feared, lest she should think her bold or inquisitive; but now she could examine it, and call it her own. But think not, gentle reader, that even this great gift could heal the wound made in that tender heart. No, a thousand gifts like that could not have been a substitute for that affection for which she pined. Hard indeed must be that unfeeling heart, that cannot bestow a kind look, word, or deed, when it will not cost a farthing; and harder still, the heart that will prevent others from bestowing them. But, reader, Fred looked to the future; he feared the loss of the (with him) precious dollar; he knew that his father intended Sabra should be brought up as their own child, and share in his large estate equally with the rest, and he was determined it should be otherwise; and Marina was always ready to assist him in trying to frustrate his father's designs; they seemed to think that to destroy the affection that existed in the family

c

towards her would be the safest way ; but this was not
an easy task, for no one, but an unreasonable selfish
person, could avoid admiring Sabra's good disposition
and amiable qualities, always yielding and submissive,
ever ready to run at every call, and constantly seeking
that affection that she was ready to bestow on every
creature : even the faithful dog and cat, the horse and
cow, were petted by her, for it was her nature to love.

After they were gone, her father said it was too bad
that she could not go,—he saw no reason for her
staying home,—it would have been as pleasant to her
as the rest.   Her mother said she felt grieved, but it
could not be helped, Fred would have his own way.
" Yes," said her father, " and I suppose he thinks he
always will, but I intend to hold the reins in my own
hands." After this conversation, Sabra went to her own
room, and gave vent to her feelings by a flood of tears.
She often found relief in this way ; she never went to
her mother with her trouble, for she did not like to hurt
her feelings.   She thought to herself, why is it that
Fred and Samuel do not love me ; she knew that her
father and mother, Jason and Asenath, loved her ; still
she did more for Samuel than for any of them, for he
wished to be waited upon ; she thought it the greatest
pleasure to perform any service they might require.
Before they returned, she became composed, and went
down stairs to assist her mother.   She endeavored to
appear as if nothing had happened.

After they returned, Henrietta asked Sabra to walk

with her, and show her the garden. When they were alone, she said: "The next time I come here on a visit, I wish you to go home with me; and we will have fine times; I have no sister, and I should like your company." Sabra was pleased with the prospect of a visit, for she had never been far from home. Henrietta told her that Jason often talked of her, and said he wished she could live with him, and go to school. The third day, they went home; Sabra often thought of them and wished that they might come again, for her father and mother said she might go with them.

Gossip was as prevalent in those days as it is at the present, and it was rumored that Jason was to be married soon. Some said his intended was a lady, and knew nothing about work; and others, that she was rich, and did not need to work; others said that she had an education, and taught school. The latter was correct. Her father died when she was quite young, leaving his widow and daughter a property sufficient for their maintenance. But gossip cannot be confined to one place, or person; every person liked Mrs. Hudson: she was the first to be sent for in sickness; always gathered herbs enough in the fall to supply all her neighbors; and people said that Sabra was just like her mother, for she knew the nature and use of every herb that grew near, and always assisted her mother in gathering them. In addition to Mrs. Hudson's good qualities, she must, of course, have bad ones; and her great besetting sin, in the eye of the commu-

nity, was her indulgence to Sabra. Everybody said
she would be a spoiled child, and this flame was constantly kept burning by Marina, who never let an
opportunity pass without leaving the impression, that
Sabra always did just as she pleased.

Nabby Merrium lived near Mrs. Hudson, and was
very sensitive, about the time she heard of an intended
marriage (her name being already placed on the old
maids' list) ; and hearing of Jason's visit, she thought
by calling upon Mrs. H., perhaps she might hear
something about Jason, or his lady ; and thought she
would gain Mrs. H's confidence, by telling her what
she heard.   After some preliminary remarks, she said :
" Mrs. Hudson, do you know what the neighbors say
about you ?" Mrs. H. replied, that she knew of
nothing in particular. " Well," continued Nabby, " they
say you are spoiling Sabra."   " Ah ! how so ?" said
Mrs. H. " By always letting her have her own way."
" Well, indeed, I do not see how I can spoil her in this
way, for she never disobeys me, never teases me, and
seldom goes from home, and she is very industrious ;
she can spin her day's work in a day, although she is
not tall enough to turn the wheel. I have to lay a
plank on the floor, raised at one end, for her to stand
upon, and she makes good yarn. She is spinning cotton
now ; I am making a long web of cotton, and I intend
she shall have her share of it, and all those plaid
blankets ; I made four of each kind, that they may each
of them have one ; I intend they shall all share alike,

and such articles as I think will be worn out, I make five that leaves one for myself: all those table-cloths and towels which you saw me making, were five of each kind, and laid by themselves. Sabra takes as much interest in the work as I do; in fact, she never deserves a reproof. If I have less trouble than other mothers with their children, I ought to be thankful, and be kind to her. It is true, she has her own way; but her way is my way, and there never was a better child. If people had said that I kept her too much confined, and that she had to work too hard, they might have some cause for saying so. I do not intend to have her work as hard always; she ought to be going to school now. For my part," said Mrs. H., " I shall pay no attention to what folks say, unless it is of more consequence."

CHAPTER XII.

THE VISIT OF MRS. HUDSON'S BROTHER.

Sabra Hudson was taught to call all Mr. and Mrs. Hudson's brothers and sisters, uncles and aunts; indeed, she knew no difference ; they all considered her a member of the family. But at this time, Mrs. Hudson had a brother visit them from a distance ; he was a large fleshy man, full of good humor and apparent mirthful-. ness.

Soon after his arrival, he said to Sabra : " And who

is this little black-eyed girl, sister ?" Mrs. Hudson replied : " she is my daughter." " But I thought you buried your daughter ?" " Not this one ;" at the same time drawing Sabra near her, and giving him a wink. They dropped the subject. Mrs. Hudson never liked to have any person allude to her adoption ; she considered Sabra her own child, and wished every one else to do so.

Sabra had not heard any allusion made to her adoption, for a long time ; she had nearly forgotten that that dear mother, she loved so fondly, was indeed not her parent, and a feeling of sadness crept over her. Her uncle was very talkative, and had a great deal to say to her. He told her, that among them, children as young as herself often became church members. He was a great singer, and went about the house and yard, singing as if very happy. At evening, he sang and prayed in the family ; his prayer was fervent and spiritual ; the tears flowed freely from Sabra's eyes, notwithstanding her effort to restrain them. After she retired, she was overwhelmed in reverie ; she thought of her loneliness, of the resolutions she had so often made to be a Christian. Thus she spent the most of the night thinking and weeping. Towards morning, she fell asleep ; and dreamed of angels and of heaven, and of an innumerable company praising God. Early in the morning, she was awakened by her uncle, passing through the hall, singing this hymn :

"A mighty love inspires my soul with sacred fires,
And animate desires, my soul to renew;
I love my blessed Jesus, on whom bright angels gaze,
And symphony increases, above the etherial blue;
And O give him glory! and O give him glory!
    For glory is his due."

The hall extended through the house, above and below, and he made it ring with melody. Devotion like this was unusual in this family : if performed at all, it must be with the utmost solemnity. There was seldom time for family prayers, except upon the Sabbath, and then Fred and Samuel never remained. They did not attend church where their father and mother did ; but attended the church that was the most popular ; and besides, their minister, Mr. A., would take supper with the young people when they had a ball. Marina was fond of dancing, and she could influence the rest whenever she chose.

During Mr. W.'s stay, he said to his sister : "Ordelia, you ought to send Sabra to school ; she has intellect, and would easily become a good scholar. I have had considerable conversation with her. She has a depth of mind seldom found in a child of her age, and would make a splendid singer ; she is quick to learn a tune, and has learned a number of me. It has taken but little time. Her voice is melodious. She ought to sing God's praises here, for God has sealed her for his own, and that child will praise Him in a fairer clime." These words affected her mother very much; she knew that Sabra's advantages were limited; and replied: " I hope Jason will send her to school, as he lives in a village."   When he was leaving, he called Sabra to him and said to her, that probably they would never meet again on the shores of time, but that they would meet beyond the grave, to praise God forever, in sweet melodious strains; and then commenced singing a beautiful hymn which he had taught her to sing.   The following is the first verse :

"My soul is full of glory, inspiring my tongue :
Could I meet with angels, I would sing them a song ;
I would sing of my Jesus, and tell of his charms,
And beg them to bear me to his loving arms."

He then bade them farewell.   Sabra often thought of him, after he was gone, and wondered why all Christians were not like him.   Their nearest neighbors, the Heulet family, had built a house, and the son who was married, lived by himself.   He was very pious, and afterwards became deacon of the church. Sabra often got permission to stay all night with Eliza ; her chief object was, that she might hear Mr. Heulet pray, for he always prayed with his family.   She would talk with Eliza about her uncle, and tell her how she wished to be a Christian.   Little did Mr. H. know the effect his prayers had upon Sabra's tender heart, or how often they caused the penitential tears of grief to flow. O ye who profess to be Christians, do your duty ; it shall be like the bread cast upon the water, which shall be found after many days. One kind sentence uttered by you in faith may take root and in after years bring forth fruit an hundred fold. Perform a good deed, speak a kind word, or merely bestow a pleasant smile, and you will receive the same in return. The happiness you bestow upon others is reflected back to your own bosoms.

CHAPTER XIII.

THE MARRIAGE OF JASON.

It was rumored about the neighborhood that Jason was married. Sabra feared that it was a mistake, but it was soon confirmed by Jason himself, who sent them word that he would visit them soon, and bring his wife. Sabra began to think about her clothes: she knew that Jason lived in the centre of a fashionable town, and she thought her dresses would look very odd; she feared that Jason and Henrietta would be ashamed of her; but had always been satisfied with her mother's choice until now, although she had often thought her taste old-fashioned. Mrs. Hudson was very economical and saving; she usually bought blue and white calico,—she thought it was the strongest, and it never faded,—and checked blue and white factory, which she thought the best for aprons. She abhorred the thought of pan-talettes: Sabra never wore any. She thought it extravagant to employ a dress-maker, and had learned to cut her own dresses (gowns she called them) ; the waist consisted of a straight piece, gathered at the bottom into the belt, and drawn with a string at the top, and straps to go over the shoulder ; two breadths with bias piece was sufficient for the skirt. You may imagine, reader, that it would look very inferior at the present day. Sabra asked her mother, if she was to have a new dress ? Her mother said, she would get her a bombazette ; and Sabra chose a light blue figured one. She asked her mother if she might get Mrs. Heulet to assist her in fitting it. Mrs. Hudson said Mrs. H. would think it very strange if she did, for Marina could fit dresses. Sabra knew that Asenath would willingly assist her, if she knew how, but she never fitted her own : she said no more, but cut it herself, allowing, as usual, for growth. She was cheered by thinking that she could induce Henrietta to fit the next dress, and instruct how to make it decently. She was careful to have all the work performed, and her apparel ready, fondly anticipating nothing but the greatest pleasure.

Ah ! disappointment, why didst thou ever have a name ? The day arrived, and they came : they were all very happy in meeting again. Henrietta said, " she supposed that Sabra was ready to go with them." She said " yes." Her mother and Asenath said it would be very lonely without her. The time they remained passed very pleasantly. Sabra was in the height of enjoyment ; she thought that even Fred smiled upon her oftener than usual ; he had been very pleasant ever since he refused to let her ride. Her mother thought she had better not commence to go to school this time, for she could not spare her long, for they were going to build, and they would require assistance at home, and the next time she might stay any longer. She felt quite grieved when she bade her father and mother good-bye, but she soon felt quite happy, for Jason was pointing out the places by the road side where he had been hunting, and the streams where he had fished. He often asked Sabra, if she would be homesick. She was very sure she should not; she could not be homesick where he was; she had never been from home, and had no idea of homesickness.

CHAPTER XIV.

SABRA'S INTRODUCTION TO MRS. HUNT.

They passed a number of villages, but none as large as the town of C., where they resided. At length they entered a beautiful village; there were splendid houses on either side of the street; there was also a large stone building, which attracted her attention; it was enclosed by a high stone wall, with iron pickets on the top, and something at the windows, she knew not what, but they were grates. She asked Jason who lived there? He informed her it was the jail, and that there were prisoners confined within, for bad conduct. This made her feel very sad, and she could think of nothing else until they drove up to their own house. They were getting out of the chaise, when Henrietta's mother, Mrs. Hunt, came to the door and assisted in carrying in the baggage, for Mrs. Hudson had supplied them bountifully with butter, cheese, lard, and a loaf of rye and Indian bread.

Henrietta said : " This is Sabra Hudson." Mrs. Hunt spoke to her, and said : " Is this the girl I have so often heard you speak of ?" Sabra thought that Mrs. Hunt viewed her from head to feet critically, and a feeling of sadness crept over her. Jason had gone to take home the carriage ; Henrietta went to an adjoining room to lay by her things. Her mother followed her, and Sabra heard her say : " Is this Jason's sister, he so often speaks of ?" " Yes," said Henrietta, " and she is a nice girl, too, mother." " Well, your associates will think you have married into a country family, sure enough ; how awkwardly she is dressed : Maria Atherton will be ashamed to associate with her ; she lives near, and is about her age." Henrietta said : " You need not be uneasy, it will all be right." Sabra heard the conversation, and being very sensitive, she could scarcely refrain from weeping. She went to the window and looked out for Jason. She soon saw him coming, and she sprang to the door to meet him. It was soon tea time, but Sabra had no appetite ; she was thinking of what Mrs. Hunt said to Henrietta. After tea, Jason was going to the shop ;

and asked Sabra to go with him. She ran for her bonnet
and shawl, but Mrs. Hunt said, " she had better stay
in the house ; she is fatigued already, and has no
appetite." Sabra was again disappointed, but she found
an interesting book, and amused herself by reading.

It soon became dark, and Mrs. Hunt said Sabra
was tired and had better go to bed. She wished, however, to sit up until Jason came in, and was told perhaps
it would be late. She had hoped that she was to sleep
alone, but Henrietta took her to the adjoining bed-room
and told her she was to sleep with her mother ; that
before she was married, she had always slept with her,
and that she chose company. Henrietta talked very
kindly to her, and told her she would call her in time
for breakfast ; that they did not rise early as they
did at father Hudson's ; and, bidding her good night,
she left her. Sabra tried to pray, but her heart was
full ; she laid herself down, but thoughts of her dear
home rushed into her mind. She thought of her dear
mother ; and although twelve hours had not yet passed
since she bade her good-by, it seemed a long, long time
to her. She wondered if the chickens and turkeys had
been fed, and who milked old *Nab* and *Sputter*, and
if the rennet had been prepared ; for, in the morning,
there would be a cheese to make. And then she thought
of those she had heard Henrietta speak of as being near
her age, Maria Atherton, Sophia Davis, and others.
She heard Mrs. Hunt come to bed, but she lay very
still that she might think her asleep. She would have

given much if she had been alone, that she might have
relieved her burdened heart by weeping. At length
she fell asleep, and dreamed that Sophia Davis and
Adaline Jones called for her to take a walk with them.
They were dressed very neatly, and looked very
genteel. She stepped out to get her bonnet; and heard
Sophia say to Adaline : " Oh, pshaw ! how awkwardly
she is dressed ; what will Sophrona Thompson and Adelaide Woodard say if they see us ?" " O never mind,"
said Adaline, " she is from the country, and they will
make allowances. For my part I do not care what
they say, I like her countenance ; she is intelligent,
and good company, I know, if she is dressed odd."
Sabra could bear no more, but commenced crying
bitterly. It awakened Mrs. Hunt, who spoke to her
and awoke her, saying : " What is the matter ? Are
you homesick already ? I told Henrietta that it would
be just so, and that you would want to go home before
twenty-four hours." Sabra composed herself as well
as she could, and told her she had been dreaming,
and was very sorry she had disturbed her. She
lay still, feeling very glad that it was a dream. In
the morning she awoke quite early, and heard Mrs.
Hunt get up ; she told Sabra to lie until Henrietta
called her, as they did not breakfast early. Their bed-
room was adjoining the kitchen, and she soon heard Mrs.
Hunt relating to Henrietta what had happened in the
night ; how she was awakened from a sound sleep, by
Sabra, and that she had not slept any since she had

been awakened ; she did not believe that Sabra was dreaming, she thought her homesick, and very likely they would have to take her back home, and that would be expensive : she thought they had better have left her at home.   Henrietta told her she thought Sabra would be contented.

Now, Mrs. Hunt was not, strictly speaking, a penurious person, but she had been a widow before, and was necessitated to economy : she had five small children when Mr. Hunt married her ; they had been educated, and gone from home.   Mr. Hunt was connected with the first class in society, and she wished to maintain the position in which he left her at his death. When Jason came, Henrietta spoke to Sabra, who was ready for breakfast ; she was glad to see Jason, and was quite cheerful ; she had determined, if she was homesick, that they should not know it.   She knew that her mother would come for her in a few weeks. Jason said, she might go to the shop with him, (he kept a jeweller's shop,) and she would see many new things to attract her attention.   Mrs. Hunt could find no reasonable excuse to keep her.   She felt quite happy while she was with him ; she saw many fine things, and Jason let her wind up the watches ; he told her, that when she was old enough to wear it he would give her one ; this pleased her very much, and in due time she obtained the watch.   While she was at the shop, there came in a gentleman, and he said : " Hudson, this is your sister, I know, for she looks just like you."

He replied, " Yes, and all the sister I have." The gentleman praised her, and Sabra felt quite proud to think that any person thought she looked like Jason, for she loved him and thought him good looking. They had some sport about it, after the man had gone. Jason said, he was not the only one that thought they looked alike ; he had often heard people making that remark.

Jason said : " it is near noon, it is time for us to go to the house." " It is only half past eleven," said Sabra, as if anxious to stay as long as possible. But Jason laid by his green baize apron, and started for the house. As he turned to the left, Sabra exclaimed : " this is not the way ;" but he replied, " I am going to show you the milliner's shop." The window was filled with hats, and rich ribbons; it was the first large milliner's shop she had ever seen. Jason said, " we will go in and see what they have got."

" Good morning, Mr. Hudson, how do you do, how is your family ? take seat, you are quite a stranger," said Miss Mulikan, the milliner's sister, all with one breath. " Good morning," replied Mr. Hudson ; "this is my sister, I called to let her see your new-fashioned hats, and to let her select one for herself." Sabra was perfectly astonished ; it would be hard to tell which surprised her most, the splendor of the hats, and the beautiful ribbons and artificials, or the idea that she was to have one herself. She was told to choose one. She accordingly selected one, but it was quite plain. Mrs. Porter, the milliner, said it was very pretty, but

not trimmed sufficiently to suit her age, and she selected a rich artificial, and Mr. Hudson told her to put
that on the hat, and it would look very well. They
left the shop, and Sabra was delighted with her present,
thinking that no one but Jason would have made her
a present like that. She wondered what Mrs. Hunt
would say. They arrived at the house, just in time
for dinner. Henrietta met them at the door, and
exclaimed: " O what a beautiful hat ! where did you
get it ?" Sabra said, that Jason bought it at Mrs.
Porter's for her; "is not he kind? it is beautiful." Sabra
showed it to Mrs. Hunt ; she said it was very pretty,
but there would be quite a contrast between that and
her other apparel. Henrietta said, we will soon have
all things correspond. After dinner, Henrietta asked
Sabra to go with her to the store. They examined
many pieces of nice goods. Sabra thought Henrietta
was going to purchase a dress for herself; but she selected one from the rest, and after having it measured
and rolled up with the trimmings, she gave it to Sabra,
who was quite surprised, and said : " There is nearly
twice as much as I usually have for a dress." Henrietta replied : " There is none too much, my dear ;
we will have it made, and I am sure you will like it."
They returned home, and Henrietta went immediately
to work at the dress. She prepared the skirt for
Sabra, and said : " Now see how well you can make
that ; not how quick you can have it done ; first learn
to do your work well, and then try to get along as fast
as you can." D

Sabra never forgot this remark; she had not heard it before; it became very useful to her afterwards. Henrietta fitted the waist, and it sat neatly; the next day they finished it, and Sabra put it on. Henrietta told her to wear it the remainder of the day; it was Saturday. At night, when she went to bed, she felt quite sad. She had not, during the week, learned her verses as usual; she could not sleep, but wished she lay alone, that she might indulge in weeping; this, she thought, would relieve her burdened mind. It was quite late when she awoke next morning, but she did not hear any person up. After a long time, she thought she would get up and make a fire, and perhaps get breakfast. She arose, but Mrs. Hunt told her not to get up, that it was Sunday; there was no use in rising early, for they did not attend church.

Sabra was in the habit of rising as early on the Sabbath as any other day, and she thought of the hymn she had so often repeated : " This is the day the Lord arose, so early from the dead," &c. She thought of many other verses which she had recited at the Sabbath-school. When she heard them up, she was very glad, for the sun was shining brightly. After breakfast the bell began to ring, and afterwards to toll. Sabra felt quite sad; she had not been accustomed to hear the bell toll, for there was none where she attended church. Henrietta called her to take a seat with her by the window, to see the people go to church, that she might see how they were dressed, &c. Jason had acquired the habit of staying from church in consequence of ill health, and was not urged by his parents afterwards; consequently it became a habit. He used to spend his Sabbaths reading, as did Henrietta, also; they were both exceedingly fond of reading. Henrietta gave Sabra an interesting book, but she soon thought of home and the Sabbath-school. There was Henrietta Heulet, and Eliza P.,—they would recite their verses, and perhaps would get ahead of her; and there was Thaddeus and Theodore Saunderson—they might excel her in number of verses; they always attended church. She came to the conclusion that she would commit to memory as many verses as possible, perhaps her teacher would hear them, after she returned home, and credit them. She took her Bible and commenced her studies. She committed a large number of verses, but the day seemed very long, and often did she wish she was at home, that she might see her mother. She thought how foolish she had been, to anticipate so much pleasure in being away from home; took her book and went to the garden, where she found a retired place, seated herself, and wept bitterly. She looked at the cheerful hen that was picking seeds, and thought it a happy creature, enjoying itself with the luxury of contentment; and would gladly have exchanged beings with it; but no. She thought herself a subject of sorrow.

After tea, Jason asked Henrietta and Sabra to take a walk. They ascended a hill in rear of the town, where they could have a view of the whole village. Jason

showed Sabra where a battle had been fought in the
revolutionary war.   She had many questions to ask
and was quite interested. The next morning Henrietta
was preparing to wash ; for she always observed the
good old custom of washing on Monday.   Sabra was
anxious to assist her, but she chose to do the washing
alone.   She told Sabra that she might do the chamber
work ; this pleased her, for she liked to make beds, to
sweep and dust.   After she had done this neatly, she
went down and enquired for something more to do.
Mrs. Hunt asked her if she found any pins while sweep-
ing, and what she had done with them.   Now, Sabra
was always careful to look in the dirt for paper, rags,
and pins, when she swept ; but she had not been particular to put the pins upon the cushion, as she should
have done, but had put them upon her dress.   Mrs.
Hunt told her she should have put them upon the
cushion.   Sabra felt quite ashamed that she had been
so careless, and told her she would recollect the next
time to put them in their proper place.

Towards evening, Maria Atherton and Adelaide
Woodard called for Sabra to take a walk. She thought
immediately of her dream, but she was happily disappointed, for she found they were not proud or particular,
and she knew they were not ashamed of her on account
of her dress. They went to the shop. Jason was glad to
see them, and showed them some nice jewellery. They
went round the mill pond, and back to the house.
Sabra began to enjoy her visit, and to feel more con-

tented; but there seemed to be one obstacle in the way; she could not please Mrs. Hunt. She did not know why it was, for she tried more to please her than any of the other members of the family, and she was always respectful to the aged.

Henrietta was very kind to Sabra, and taught her to do many things which she had not been accustomed to do, such as making button holes, darning stockings, and other things which she had been in the habit of getting her mother to do for her. Sabra could perform all these very neatly, and thought there was no person like Henrietta. She felt quite contented until Sunday came—it was so unlike her Sabbath at home. She thought of her Sabbath-school teacher, of her class-mates, of Thaddeus and Theodore, and then applied herself to her lesson, determined that they should not excel her in verses. But her heart was full, and she had to find a retired place, and relieve her troubled spirit by a flood of tears.

CHAPTER XV.

MR. AND MRS. HUDSON, OR THE FOLKS AT HOME.

Mr. and Mrs. Hudson felt quite lonely without Sabra ; neither of them mentioned it to the other, each waiting for the other to mention the subject first. One morning Mr. Hudson came in and said : " Mrs. Hud-

son, when do you intend to have Sabra to return home ?
It is very lonely here without her ; I tell you there is
one missing when she is gone.   I find she is a great
help to me as well as to you.   She was always ready
to turn the grindstone for me if I required it, and many
other services she performs for me, which I did not
think of when she was here ; but the fact is, I miss her
every day.   I think we had better go after her some
day this week."   Mrs. Hudson was very glad, for she
was afraid Sabra would be homesick, for she had never
been from home before.   She said she could go the
next day, and it was decided that they should start the
next morning.

We will now return to Sabra, who felt quite sure that
they would come for her that week, and she often stood
at the window looking for them.   She happened to be
there when they came, and she ran to the door to meet
them, as much pleased as if she had not seen them for
months.   She had much to relate to them during their
ride home, but she did not like to tell them that she had
been homesick.

Asenath met them at the door, and was glad to see
Sabra, who thought they all appeared pleasant; and
she felt quite happy in being at home again.

Saturday she had everything prepared for the Sabbath.   She took off the artificials from her new hat;
perhaps she thought they would not please her Sabbath-
school teacher ; maybe she thought that Theodore
would think her vain; be that as it may, she thought

them too gay. Sabbath morning came : it was a beautiful morning; one of those mornings that appear to the thoughtful mind as though nature itself was praising God. She went to church with her father and mother, with a joyful heart.

When she had recited her usual number of verses, she requested her teacher to hear her recite those verses she had committed while absent. Her teacher said he would hear a part of them then, and the rest next Sabbath. On Monday, she applied herself to her work as usual ; and was always happy when she thought she pleased the family. She often wished she could please Fred and Marina as easily as she could them. The fact was this, the love of approbation was promiment in her phrenological development. She went to school during the short winter term, but could not find any time to study or read at home, for the knitting was always ready; and besides this, her mother told her, that when she had finished her knitting she might knit for herself, and she would find yarn.

During that winter, card-playing became an amusement for the evenings. Sabra's mother feared she would learn, and acquire a love for it. She promised to give her twenty dollars when she was eighteen, if she would not play. Sabra very willingly promised, for she did not think it was right, and she had no desire to play.

During the winter, they were preparing material for building; the next season the house was finished, and they moved into it. Sabra had a nice room by herself, and a closet for her clothes. Nothing in particular happened, until the birth of Fred's oldest child. Asenath came and told Sabra that Marina had a little boy. She was very much pleased, for she thought they would let her nurse it. Many thoughts rushed though her mind, and new hopes sprang up in her sensitive heart. She would love the babe, and they would love her.

She cleared off the breakfast table, and requested Asenath to look at her cheese curd; for she was making cheese, and her mother had not been at home, but was with Marina. Asenath thought she was getting along finely. " I shall get you or mother to look at it before I put it in the press," said Sabra. Asenath said she would come; and then went home. She worked away with a light heart, until she thought her cheese curd was sufficiently drained, and then went to call Asenath, who lived in the first part of the house. As she came near the door, she met Fred; he spoke very harshly to her, asking what she was going there for; he said she had no business there, that it was no place for her. His words sank to the botton of her heart, as the stone sinks to the bottom of the fountain; it crushed all her hopes, and brought tears to her eyes. She endeavored to tell him her errand, but he waited not to hear it. Asenath heard Fred: she went to the door and said, it was unkind for Fred to speak so harshly. She went home with her, and tried to comfort her; but Sabra could not forget it, for it had been a long time since he had spoken crossly to her. She assisted in putting the cheese in the press, and then went home, leaving Sabra alone.

Towards noon, her mother came home, and told her that they had got a babe for to nurse, and that it would be company for her. Sabra felt very differently from what she did, when Asenath told her. Her mother saw there was something wrong, and asked what was the matter. Sabra told her what Fred said. Her mother said it was wrong for Fred to scold her, but that she might go, and see the babe. Sabra said she did not wish to go, and it was some time before she consented. When she went, Fred and Marina were glad to see her.

CHAPTER XVI.

JASON AND HENRIETTA'S LITTLE DAUGHTER.

They had heard of the birth of their child, and no one desired to see it as did Sabra. It was two or three months older than Willie; and Sabra was looking for them, for they sent word they were coming to visit them. The day arrived, and Sabra was watching for them. She met them at the door. Jason took the babe from the chaise and said : " I will give this to you, Sabra; it is your little niece." Sabra exclaimed: " What a pretty babe! What is its name? It should be Henrietta,

but they say it is Hattie ; we must call you that, I suppose." She loved Willie exceedingly, but she thought
Fred and Marina were not desirous that she should
love him; for it was always, " take care," " you will
hurt him," or " that will do." She often wished that
she could caress him, as freely as she did her kitten.
She knew it would not be so with Jason and Henrietta ;
they would permit her to love Hattie, as much as she
chose ; and she did love her exceedingly, and was never
homesick, when at Jason's afterwards.

When Willie was four or five months old, Marina was
very glad to have Sabra take care of him.   She even
condescended to hire her.   She had a pattern muslin
dress, for a ball dress, and it was quite too small for her,
and of no use.   She said she would allow her half a
dollar a week for her services, until she had paid for that
dress if she desired it. Her mother consented, but she
was to come home at night to sleep. Sabra used every
exertion to please, and worked very hard ; often got very
tired, for Marina was a great worker, but she was
pleased with the idea of earning the dress herself, and
would not complain until she had paid for it.

CHAPTER XVII.

THE EXPLOSION.

One winter's day, Marina asked Sabra if she would
stay from school and take care of Willie, for she had

to bake. Sabra was always pleased when asked to take
care of him, and willingly consented. Marina was making pies, and Willie was in the cradle, front of the
oven. Sabra took him up, but he reached around to
see the fire blazing in the brick oven ; he was crowing
and cooing, but Sabra thought the fire shone too brightly in his face, and moved him from before it ; and
fortunately, for immediately there was a terrible noise,
like a burst of thunder, and the room was filled with
smoke. With great presence of mind, Sabra gave the
babe to its mother, and commenced moving articles of
wearing apparel, which were on fire, out of the window,
which was broken in pieces ; they had been ironing, and
there were may things left to air ; the cradle pillow and
linen were all on fire ; these she threw out of the window, and then went out and covered them with snow.
They then started for the other house, for it so happened
that there was no person else in the house, when they met
their mother coming up, who had heard the noise but supposed it to be nearer. She told them that it was powder
undoubtedly. Sabra turned back with her mother ;
they found a desolate-looking room,—the smoke had
disappeared, and the fire was extinguished, except some
coals which were scattered on the hearth, the pan of
flour was scattered on the floor, one door broken, the
side of the room split off, and the window entirely broken
to pieces. They went up stairs ; there was no fire there,
but the closet was fractured, and that part of the house
looked wretched. They put things in order, as well

as they could, and went to see Marina and Willie, who had gone to the other house. Willie had screamed frightfully, but they supposed him only frightened, but Marina had discovered two blisters upon his face,— this was all the injury they had sustained. Fred had purchased a tin canister of powder, and had placed it in the oven to dry, some days previous to the explosion, and had forgotten to remove it. On that day he was from home, and did not return until the next day. He thought it a miraculous preservation, that either of their lives was spared. Marina said, that poor little Willie would surely have been killed, if it had not been for aunty, for she had just removed him from the cradle. It was but seldom that she called Sabra aunt, to the child, but this time it was uttered easily. Sabra felt a thrill of joy pass through her soul; she thought, "Perhaps they may love me now as I have saved Willie's life."

That night was a solemn one to Sabra; she thought how narrowly she had escaped death, and could not sleep; she thought if she had died, her soul would have been lost; and felt that she was less prepared than ever. She prayed as she had often done before, that God would change her heart, and forgive her sins. She knew that she had often grieved his spirit, and said, go thy way for this time. She had even gone so far, as to join in the giddy dance. She thought of her happy uncle, of the revival of religion, but professors had become lukewarm, and the subject of religion was seldom mentioned. She knew that her mother was always thoughtful, but, alas! she had no abiding evidence of her acceptance with Christ. Her father always kept up family prayers upon the Sabbath, and sometimes during the week if it was convenient. She desired to possess that religion, that would make her an every-day Christian ; but childhood and youth are vanity, and her convictions gradually wore away.

CHAPTER XVIII.

THE SINGING SCHOOL.—SAMUEL'S SICKNESS, &C.

Late in the fall of the year, Sabra went to reside with Jason, with the intention of going to school. She had not commenced, when her father sent for her. The society were to have a singing school : some of then told Mr. Hudson that he ought to send for Sabra, that she might learn music ; they said she had a good voice, and would be a great acquisition to the choir. He accordingly sent for her. Sabra was very glad to have the privilege of learning to sing, for she had a good ear for music, and was passionately fond of singing. They had a good teacher, one who taught the rules thoroughly. Here she met with her Sabbath-school mates. Thaddeus and Theodore attended the school.

Asenath's sister, Emma Morris, was living with her, and attended the school. She became an excellent

singer.   Emma and Sabra were often asked to sing
duets.   At the close of the school, the teacher said
he wished to have the choir organized, and their lead-
ers chosen for each part ; they accordingly met for
that purpose.   Emma and Sabra were chosen to lead
the soprano.   They were both surprised at this, for
they did not think themselves competent.   Mr. Hudson felt quite proud of Sabra's attainments ; he knew
her services would be valuable in the choir, and he
was one of the first to sustain the society.   The credit
of her assistance belonged to himself, for he had bought
her singing book, and paid the expense of her tuition.
Soon after this, there was a singing school in the town
of B.   Mr. Hudson thought he would send Sabra to
this school also, if he could find a suitable place for
her, where she could earn her board during the term.
It was three miles from his residence.   He went to
make inquiries respecting the school, and had no trouble
in obtaining a boarding-place for her, for her services.
Sabra was well pleased with the teacher and the school,
but the society was more fashionable there, and she
often felt annoyed on account of her dress : for although
her apparel was sometimes of rich material, yet
it was not made after the latest fashion ; for this cause,
some of the scholars slighted her ; others, of better
judgment, treated her politely.

We might here remark, that parents and guardians,
who are able, should not subject those under their
control to ridicule, by dressing them so very differently

from others; it frequently causes them to appear singularly awkward. Attending this school, introduced Sabra into new society; she afterwards attended parties in the village; and her convictions upon the subject of religion became less frequent. During her attendance at this school, she became thoroughly competent to read music. Much care was taken, by her father and mother, that she might acquire this accomplishment, while other branches of her education were neglected.

After the school closed, and Sabra had returned home her brother Samuel had a severe attack of the bilious cholic. The physician had little hope of his recovery. Sabra remained with him night and day; Asenath was with him also, but she had no confidence in her own abilities. She was willing to render any service she might be able to perform, if conscious that it would not be injurious. Samuel had taken a large quantity of calomel, and when he began to recover, his mouth was very sore, and required washing often. This Sabra did, and also prepared all his food. She could broil a steak to suit his taste, better than any other person. His bed was not right, unless she made it. His medicine was not rightly mixed, unless she prepared it. In fact nothing was done exactly right if not performed by Sabra, and she took great pleasure in pleasing him. From this time until Sabra married, she always took care of him, whenever he was sick; and he was often afflicted with the same distressing disease.

About this time, Samuel, who was not very partial to farming, engaged in the manufacture of an article that was extensively made in some parts of the same town. In order to accomplish it successfully, it required a water power. He commenced with a foot lathe. Part of this business was usually performed by females, and he employed Emma Morris. There was a small stream passing near the house ; Samuel thought a dam might be constructed, to keep back the water ; it would only overflow a few acres of land, and the power would be sufficient. He did not wish to incur the expense of building unless his father would give him a deed of the land. He urged his father to do so, but he refused. Samuel informed Sabra that his father had refused the deed, and that he had almost concluded to move away. Sabra could not bear the idea of their moving ; she thought she would ask her father, why it was that Samuel could not have it. She told him that Samuel wished to build. Her mother was present, and joined in the persuasion. Mr. Hudson replied : " I shall deed no land to any person, during my lifetime, and they need not expect it. I intend," said he to Mrs. Hudson, " the children shall have all my property, equally divided, after my decease, and there will be enough for all of them. I hope each of them will be satisfied with their portion ; you recollect the promise I made you when you were sick ; I intend to fulfil it, or leave you able to fulfil it. The children are now young, and can help themselves ; it will be just as useful to them, to receive it at a future time as to have it now. If Samuel wishes to build, I have no objections to make, but he must run the risk of losing it ; I shall not assist him at present." They were sorry that Samuel could not have it, as his own property. Sabra told Samuel what their father had said. He replied : " Perhaps it will make little difference ;" and with his father's consent, he built a workshop, and employed a number of hands.

CHAPTER XIX.

MRS. HUNT'S DEATH.

Mrs. Hunt was taken ill, and lived but a short time. After her death, Henrietta was very lonely ; she sent for Sabra, who went immediately, for they all sympathized with Henrietta. During the time she remained there, she went to school. She was now, what some would call an interesting, handsome young lady ; eyes beaming with intelligence, her form slender and genteel ; and, with many, here will commence the most interesting part of her history.

She had thoroughly studied the subject of flirtation, and had fully decided, never to receive particular attention from any gentleman, merely to have it said she had a beau, or to pass away time. She became acquainted with the young people here, and had many friends,

E

particularly among the singers; was invited to the choir, and assisted in leading the singing in church. Here she became acquainted with a gentleman of pleasing manners and of good reputation. He was a particular friend of Henrietta's. He offered Sabra his hand in marriage. She became almost persuaded to accept his offer, and probably would have done well if she had, as he appeared attached to her, and also pleased her friends ; but she decided differently. She knew that his religious sentiments were very different from her own, and although fully aware that she was not a Christian, yet she intended to be one; and she intended to find a partner who would lead her on, rather than retard her progress in the Christian course. She was very tenacious of the opinions she entertained ; and we will say here, that she had seldom been compelled to yield to any decision but her own ; hence she was wilful, and very much set in her own way. There was more than one reason why she did not accept Mr.—'s offer ; she had heard him take the name of God in vain, and it was painful to her ; yet notwithstanding all this she esteemed him highly as a friend, and recollected him with respect. While we are speaking of offers of marriage, we may here speak of one more, which soon succeeded the first. He was a gentleman of great respectability, a member of one of the best families, very precise in his address, genteel in his appearance, and evidently as set in his own opinion as was Sabra. He was strictly moral, and this was the creed of his religion. His manners were pleasing to her. He was some years older than herself. She thought she would consider the subject. She often conversed with him upon the subject of religion and expressed her desire to become a Christian. He endeavored to convince her that she was already all that the Scriptures required. She had been persuaded to attend a large military ball ; and when the captain led up his fair lady to open the ball, many exclaimed, " what a handsome couple !" But her heart was not joyful, and she thought she would never attend another ball.

It was not many weeks before he insisted upon her attending another party. She begged to be excused, but he urged her ; she inquired why he wished for a companion for life that did not enjoy this amusement. He finally told her if she would go this time, he would never urge her again. She consented, and sure enough, he never did ask her again, neither did Sabra ever dance after that evening. Her convictions were revived during the evening ; and while upon the floor, she was so much overcome with a sense of guilt that she was unable to end the cotillion, but begged her partner to excuse her, and took her seat. She soon told a particular female friend how she felt, and they left the room, and went by themselves ; this friend had similar feelings, and they both resolved never to dance again. Everything appeared very solemn to them, and they never again entered a ball-room. At an early hour they left. On their way home, Sabra told M. W., that she had fully determined never to attend another ball, that she intended to seek religion. He commended her for her resolution, said it was not much pleasure after all, that he could enjoy an evening at home as well.

About this time, the Rev. Mr. Southmaid (who afterwards became a missionary, and perished with hunger among the heathen,) was holding a protracted meeting in the town of C., where he preached; he held what were called inquiry meetings. Sabra attended them; she was burdened with a sense of guilt, and her sins were as mountains before her, yet her heart rebelled against God. She was tempted to think, that God, being almighty, might have ordained some other way to save sinners, without the suffering of Christ. Mr. Southmaid always dwelt upon the subject of the atonement, and the sufferings of Christ; it had been his subject during that day. Sabra knew very well that the fault was in her own wicked heart, but still the rebellious principle was there. She said to Henrietta, going to church, that she hoped the minister would have some other subject that evening. She tried to pray, that her feelings might be right; and as she walked to the church, her thoughts were entirely upon the subject. Mr. S. read the hymn, commencing with this line:

"Alas! and did my Saviour bleed?"

She tried to sing with the rest of the choir, but her heart was too heavy. The minister made an excellent prayer, and afterwards commenced reading the second chapter of Hebrews; as he read, her heart began to soften; when he reached the 16th verse, a ray of light from above burst into her soul: the plan of salvation looked plain; she was perfectly happy. The whole chapter seemed new; she felt indeed like a new creature. She did not think that she had experienced religion at this time, or any change of heart, only a change in her feeling, in regard to the plan of salvation. She now thought nothing but Omnipotent Wisdom could have devised a way so plain to restore lost humanity : that our Saviour had taken upon himself our nature, having come to redeem us, and showed our wandering feet the way. The path to heaven looked very plain, so much so, that a wayfaring man, though a fool, need not err therein. She enjoyed the meeting very much. When asked if she intended to be a Christian, she answered, yes, but did not tell of the change in her feelings during the evening; if she had, she might have been encouraged to hope in the mercy of God. She went home very happy ; told Henrietta how differently she felt, how happy she then was, and of her intention to become a Christian. The next day, she called upon a Christian friend, Mrs. D., and told her what a change there was in her mind. Mrs. D. told her she had experienced religion. Sabra could not believe it ; she expected some greater manifestation of Divine power ; and through her unbelief, her happy feelings wore away, but her convictions remained, and she lived in the faithful discharge of her duties, without a good hope in Christ, for nearly two years.

———

CHAPTER XX.

SAMUEL AND ASENATH'S ELDEST CHILD.

Spring had returned, with all its cheering beauty, and Sabra had returned home. Samuel and Asenath's eldest daughter was called Eveline. A nurse was obtained, who was called skilful, but she would not allow Asenath sufficient food to strengthen her. Asenath said to Sabra, " I shall rejoice when I am able to go to the kitchen and help myself to food. I am often faint and hungry, but nurse will not allow me more ; she says food will create fever." Sabra returned home, and told her mother, and inquired if she might prepare some palatable nourishment and carry it to Asenath. Her mother replied, " Yes, dear ; I always thought you would have been a better nurse for her than Mary. Get whatever you think proper, and carry it up the back stairs." Sabra made some light pancakes, and some nice tarts, and a dish of tea, and carried them to Asenath, and told her that she had brought her a lunch. Asenath thought it was excellent. Every day, Sabra would slip up the back stairs with her server laden with something which she thought Asenath would relish, always having something different, that her appetite might not become satiated by having a similar dish each day. Asenath often spoke of it afterwards, and said she never had her food taste as good as it did then. It may be remarked here, that they never had any hard thoughts of each other, but always esteemed each other, as sisters ; and a thrill of joy would always enter the heart of Sabra, whenever Asenath called her sister.

There were now three little children in the family for Sabra to love. Willie was a sweet child, and it was difficult for her to tell which of the three she loved most. She could love Hatty more freely than Willie, for she knew it pleased Jason and Henrietta. Her time was divided between the two places. Henrietta was lonely, and her mother was willing she should remain there, when she could be spared from home, for Jason furnished nearly all her wearing apparel, and she often earned small sums herself. Jason gave her a valuable watch, and other presents.

CHAPTER XXI.

THE DISMISSAL OF MR. WARREN, AND HIS DEATH.

The manly appearance, and the genteel deportment, together with the good morals of Mr. Warren, had gained the favor of all the Hudson family. Sabra had become quite attached to him, but there was a vast difference in their manners. Sabra was free and social with both sexes; her heart was pure and unsuspecting, never watching for faults in others, and not having any fears of others watching her.

But, alas! for fallen, depraved human nature, how often do we find within the heart a disposition to calumniate or to destroy the peace of others. Sabra scarcely knew that feelings of this kind were ever veiled within the human heart. How should she, with but little experience, and never having the privilege of reading, except a few books. She had never read the Olive Branch weekly. No, it was not published then; if she had, she might have been wiser. She was tenacious of her rights, seldom crossed in her wishes; generally having her own way, she was unaccustomed to discipline. Her father and mother, both being very indulgent, she being strongly attached to them, it was her wish to please them; yet she might be called wilful and somewhat self-conceited. She was often the confidential friend of both sexes; was always careful never to divulge secrets, and always managed to keep out of disputes or difficulties. William was regarded in his father's family, somewhat as Samuel was in their family. His brothers and sisters regarded him more like a superior than an equal; they all seemed to be afraid of offending him. His youngest brother, Philander, was waiting upon a lady, and he thought William was disposed. He thought Sabra would know; accordingly he confided the subject to her, wish-

ing her to find out what William thought of it.
William saw them talking together, and jealousy,
that fatal destroyer of all happiness, entered his
peaceful heart : and not knowing whom he had to
deal with, he very abruptly asked Sabra what she
and Philander were conversing about ; and hastily
said, if she liked Philander the best, she might marry
him. This was the first unpleasant word he had ever
spoken to her. It was like the bursting of electric
fluid, which shivers the tree to atoms. She trembled
with indignation, but, as they had no opportunity then
for an explanation, they each possessed their own feelings. Sabra retired that night at an early hour, no
one knowing her trouble. She was glad to be alone,
that she might find relief in tears. Alas ! thought she,
is this human nature ? Is this the fruit of love and
friendship ? Was this from him, who seemed to watch
my every motion with delight ; who had seemed to think
me perfection itself? She prayed God to support her
in this trying hour. She made resolutions, and amended
them, but finally concluded that after an explanation she would discard all thoughts of him ; hard indeed
was the struggle in her mind. Her friends thought
she was sick, and would have called a physician, but
she said it was a severe attack of the nervous head-
ache, that she would soon be better. Four days elapsed
before the explanation. William called to see her.
Sabra was calm and decided. He inquired why she
was melancholy ; if it was in consequence of what he

had said respecting his brother.   Sabra replied : " I think that is a sufficient cause to make me feel sad." She then related to him the inquiry his brother wished her to make respecting his opinion of the lady before mentioned. William appeared very sorry ; hoped she would forgive him. He said all that was necessary to make amendment ; but it was evident that a link was broken in friendship's chain that could not .be immediately repaired. Soon after this, he was taken ill. He informed Sabra that he thought of consulting a physician who lived near her father's that he should see her parents, and ask their consent to marriage.   Sabra felt quite indignant, and replied : " You had better obtain my consent.   If my affections are regained, it will require time, and I shall be offended if you mention the subject to them." Sabra began to think that it was excitement that made him speak thus hastily to her, and that all would be right ; and she was as cheerful as ever.

All would have passed on smoothly, had not another circumstance occurred, which happened at the singing school, a few weeks afterwards.   William was a musician, and played the bass viol.   Sabra thought all was harmony when he was present, for they could keep better time.   That evening, in particular, she felt a sort of pride when she heard their singing eulogized, accompanied by his splendid bass, for he was an excellent musician.   A Mr. Miles was present that evening, a celebrated singer ; he was invited to join the choir. Sabra, as usual, sat at the end of the seat, and they gave Mr. Miles a seat beside her. She had met him at another school, and had sang with him often. He was quite sociable; he was a married man, and Sabra thought William would not object to her enjoying a friendly conversation. At intermission, he came not as usual to her seat; she wondered why, for he was well acquainted with Mr. M., and a feeling of sadness crept over her joyful heart; but when they commenced singing, her gloom dispersed, and she was happy as ever. William had accompanied her to the school that evening; but, at the close, he said nothing to her, but started with his bass viol and candle. Sabra stepped to his side, and offered to take the candle. He answered her abruptly, by saying he could carry it himself. He passed on through the crowd, and soon disappeared. Sabra felt somewhat annoyed, but it did not affect her as did the first shock; her mind was better prepared, and she thought he was displeased because she sang and conversed with Mr. Miles. She had determined to act natural, as formerly, let the consequence be as it might. She would not practice deceit. That which had appeared to her like gold, had begun to grow dim. She determined not to change her natural deportment for any man; no, not she. And she fully decided, from that hour, that she would be disengaged, the first opportunity, if indeed the cause of his neglect was what she had surmised. She then told Henrietta all her trouble; what had happened a

few weeks before, and what her intentions were in
future. Henrietta was astonished. She tried to
persuade her not to be too hasty, but to consider, or
she might regret it; but the decision had been made,
and the sacrifice completed, and she would never
again pass through the same trial. He might find a
companion as precise and polite as himself if he chose.
She could not avoid thinking how happy she had been
before the first reproval; but that was passed, and
alas ! there was no fond anticipation for her in the
future. She cared not for his wealth, or his position
in society, so long as he possessed a narrow, con-
tracted mind. Her views of morality and virtue were
high and sacred ; and she thought petty circumstances
had nothing to do with things of this order : if so, ease
of manners and familiarity was a virtue. The more
she conversed with Henrietta, and the more she
thought upon the subject, the more decided she became.
William was thinking, at the same time, that the next
confession would be made by Sabra ; but he found
himself mistaken. The gentle, loving girl was now
the firm, decided lady. The next time he came to
see her, she received him very coolly. He asked her
if he had offended her by his treatment the last time
they met. She replied that she was disgusted. He
said he thought he would give her an opportunity to
accept other company if she chose. She told him
plainly that it was her choice, and that she did not
wish him to trouble himself to accompany her again.

This was not what he expected; but he found all his expostulations and entreaties were in vain. His confession, and even tears, were of no avail; her mind was fixed. She wished him to think of her as a friend, and nothing more; said she should always entertain friendly feelings towards him and his family. He asked her what she thought people would say. She said she cared not what they said, so long as she felt justified in the course she had taken. She did not intend to sacrifice her own happiness for the favor of public opinion. She told him she was going home soon, and they would not see each other often, and the sooner the past was forgotten, the better. He urged for a correspondence, but all in vain. She requested him never to visit her again, unless it was as a friend.

Soon after this conversation, Sabra went home. She related all the conversation to her mother; told her frankly of her decision and disengagement. She, too, was as surprised as Henrietta had been, and gave her a similar caution; told her she was afraid she had been too hasty—that William had asked their consent to the marriage during her absence, but that she thought at the time that he appeared as though all was not right; and that her father told him he should not oppose her wishes in that respect if it was her choice. To this he made no reply. Her mother said: "My child, I am afraid you will not always be as fortunate as you have been; you have not had trouble like many others; but you will remember that every spoke in the wheel must come up." Sabra could not fully comprehend how this could apply to her; she thought that she had already seen trouble enough, and she was fondly anticipating more happiness in the future; but, alas! we know but little in youth what awaits us in maturer age. As adverse circumstances occurred, she often realized the truth of this saying, " that every spoke in the wheel must come up."

A few days after this, they received intelligence of a fatal accident which occurred while raising an academy in the town of M——. They had obtained men from a distance; and, among the rest, Mr. Warren was there. After the frame was nearly raised, a support gave way at the foundation, and a number of persons were precipitated among the timbers at the bottom. A number were buried, but none fatally injured except William. When he was removed from among the timber it was found that one leg was broken and badly fractured. He was carried to a house near by, where he received every attention which it was possible for friends to bestow. His mother and sister were sent for, and attended him until he died. He lingered a few days, enduring with Christian patience and fortitude the most excruciating sufferings, and then expired. His removal caused a vacuum in society, and he was very much lamented by a large circle of friends.

At the time the accident occured, Sabra was watching by the bedside of her mother, who had just been attacked by the pleurisy. The intelligence affected her very much; she was fearful that her mother would not recover, and this made her very sorrowful. The second day, she heard that William was not expected to live; also that his physician bled him, and that the bandage became loose, and the wound bled profusely, and was not discovered until it was seen dropping upon the floor. Mrs. Hudson's physician had just bled her; and Sabra was fearful lest a similar accident might occur to her, and she kept awake during the whole succeeding night, and often examined her mother's arm, to see if all was right. Mrs. Hudson did not recover until after the death and burial of Mr. Warren. Sabra did not attend his funeral, or see him during his sickness, in consequence of her mother's illness. The day after his burial, his father repaired to the boarding-house, to obtain the wearing apparel of the deceased. He unlocked his chest, and, upon the top of his clothes, he found a letter directed to Sabra; it was not sealed. His father read it; it was very affecting, and displayed a heart full of tenderness and regret. He sent it to her, and afterwards visited her himself.

CHAPTER XXII.

MISCELLANEOUS SUBJECTS.

From the time previously referred to, when Sabra experienced the change in her feelings, with regard to the plan of salvation, she was considered an humble, devoted Christian; there was a visible change in her deportment; but still she was like Christian, who had set out for the Celestial city, and while climbing the hill of difficulty had lost his roll or evidence. There were some of her associates who had experienced religion and united with the church. When Sabra saw them go forward and partake of the Holy Sacrament, and the ordinance of baptism, she felt that she was left alone. She could not tell why she was not a Christian; her mind was calm, and she felt willing to make any sacrifice, but still she had no evidence of her acceptance with God. After her mother had recovered, Jason came visit them, and she returned with them. While she was there, their second daughter was born. They called her Sabra, after her aunt. This pleased Sabra very much, and she loved the child exceedingly, and always enjoyed herself while there.

A few months before his death, William had bought a watch of Jason, and he informed Sabra he would take it back and present it to her, if his friends wished, but Mr. Warren came to pay for it, while Sabra was there. Jason told them what he had said to Sabra, but Mr. Warren wished to keep it himself; said he would never part with it. He gave Sabra some choice articles as keepsakes, he also gave her the value of the watch in money; and Jason gave her the money that he had just received from Mr. W. Sabra felt rich; she had never possessed as much money before, and she knew

her mother was saving money, in half dollars, to give
her when eighteen, as a fulfilment of her promise to
her for not playing cards ; and said she would not spend
it, but put it out on interest. Mr. Warren insisted
upon her going home with him and visiting the family.
She had never been there, and felt diffident about
going ; however, she went and enjoyed herself very
well. Mrs. Warren was a kind, motherly woman, and
Sabra always loved her afterwards. They had rich
family relatives who resided in Boston, and who lived in
style beyond her imagination. She visited there with
the family. She had never been in the city before ; and
she saw many curiosities :but nothing seemed so splendid as the furniture of P.'s house, where they visited ; it
had been selected in London, without any regard to
expense. The sofas were covered with silk velvet plush,
the carpets were as soft as down, and the mirrors large .
and splendid. It was here she formed new ideas of
aristocracy. She found the inmates of the family hospitable and kind, affable and entertaining. She saw
none of that pride and haughtiness which she expected
the rich and fashionable possessed, and she never
changed her views, although she has found some exceptions. Previous to this, she had always felt a sort of
bashfulness and awkward restraint, when in the presence of the rich and affluent ; but by experience she
found that it was not this class who were exacting and
precise ; but she found a class, in whose presence it
was necessary to be constantly upon the watch, com-

F

posed of those who have no material of worth or merit
of their own, to raise themselves to respectable society,
who are constantly striving to destroy the reputation
of others, and build themselves upon their ruins. There
are many who think, if they can lower one person in the
estimation of another, that they raise themselves in the
same proportion. This class is not confined to the
lower order of society, but is found among those who
think themselves aristocratic. Thus, by associating
with different grades of society, Sabra began to become acquainted with human nature.

After she had remained at Mr. Warren's a week,
Sabra thought she had better return to Jason's. She
had enjoyed herself very much. Mr. W. wished her
to remain longer. But she chose to go back to Jason's.
Being much delighted with her visit, she had much to
tell Henrietta about her visit to Mr. P.'s ; how Mr. P.
had a colored servant named Peter, who stood behind
his chair, ready to obey his orders ; that he stood there
during the time they were dining, which was two hours ;
that the table was cleared off three times : and this was
their usual style. Henrietta informed her that there
were many families in the city also lived in similar
style. "But," said Sabra, "after dinner he told
Peter to bring the children from the nursery ; there
was but one at table, and that one a daughter, named
Lucella, a beautiful girl about twelve years old ; that
the other two, a son and daughter, were not considered
old enough to come to the table, but took their meals

in the nursery, or by themselves. The children appeared perfectly delighted to come to the dining-room, where her parents and the company were enjoying fruit and nuts, and they seemed as pleased to see Peter as any one, and would climb up and straighten his curly locks ; and he would roll up the white of his eye, and show his teeth."

A few days after Sabra's return, her mother came for her to go home. She said Samuel wished her to work in the shop, and that her father thought it would be a good opening for her. Samuel said he would give her a dollar and a quarter a week. Jason and Henrietta remonstrated against it, and said she ought to go to school. Jason said he would pay for her school and clothe her, but her mother said she had better go, for she could board at home, and she often wished Sabra to assist her ; and if any of them were taken sick, they *must* have her. We may remark here, that wealthy farmers are deceived by the love of gain, when they think their children are doing well for themselves because they are earning money. They often become subjected to willing slavery, and neglect the cultivation of their minds. It was so with Sabra ; for the few succeeding years were hard and laborious, with but little opportunity for cultivating her mind.

CHAPTER XXIII.

SABRA COMMENCES TO WORK FOR SAMUEL.

Sabra returned home with her mother, and, after repairing her wearing apparel, commenced her laborious servitude. It was an occupation which females were usually required to learn, ere they received a reward for their labors; but Sabra had seen Emma work, and spent much time with her, and she was somewhat qualified for the work. She found that Emma was soon to be married; and would not have her for a companion, as she expected. But she found Samuel had hired Henrietta Heulet, her old schoolmate, and that he employed another girl named Lucretia. Sabra was to take charge of all the work in the girls' department. He also had workmen and apprentices; two of. them we will here mention, as we may have cause to refer often to them in this narrative,—Jeremiah Forrester and Joel Parish. Sabra had been acquainted with Joel from her childhood; he was a Sabbath-school scholar in the same school as herself, and always attended the same church. It will be recollected, that Sabra was all this time trying to live a Christian, or, in other words, to be one. She constantly maintained daily prayer, but still she had no well-grounded hope. The following verses were often repeated or sung by her :

'Tis a point I long to know,
  Oft it causes anxious thought,—
Do I love the Lord, or no ?
  Am I His, or am I not?

Yet I mourn my stubborn will,
  Find my sin a grief and thrall ;
Should I grieve for what I feel,
  If I did not love at all ?

Sabra had a Bible which she valued more than any
other book. It had been presented her by Samuel,
soon after his recovery from a serious illness. She
always remained with him day and night, and assisted
Asenath in nursing him during his sickness. After
his recovery, he would occasionally bestow a present
upon Sabra for her services. She usually kept this
Bible accessible, that she might read a few verses if
she had leisure. She had been employed by Samuel
a number of weeks, and he appreciated her services,
particularly the care she manifested that nothing
should be destroyed by negligence. She was also a
favorite among her shopmates. They placed confidence
in her ; if either of them wished to be absent, they
would desire Sabra to ask permission of Samuel. She
often found it a difficult task to keep harmony existing
between them, for they were different in their disposi-
tions. Henrietta Heulet was very mild-tempered, but
a great hector. She was constantly teasing Lucretia by
every trifling affair. Lucretia, being somewhat passion-
ate, was unable to exercise the virtue of patience, and
they would refer their disputes to Sabra for a decision,

Sabra realized her need of pious company. She had no one to converse with her upon the subject of religion ; nearly all employed by Samuel were worldly-minded and disposed to ridicule religion. Some of them had pious parents, but they had been led astray. Sabra lacked confidence in her ability to speak in the cause, and she chose not to argue the subject. She could refer to her Bible ; she had taken it with her to the shop, as her only counsellor. For some time she kept it concealed. One day she had a few leisure moments, and had been reading, and laid it upon the bench. Samuel came and saw the Bible lying there, and took it up. He appeared quite displeased ; said he was astonished ; asked who brought it there. Sabra told him she did. He said it was no place for books ; that he did not pay them for their time to read. She seldom said anything back, but at this time she felt it would be right. She restrained her emotions until after he was gone, and then burst into a flood of tears. At night, she took her Bible to the house, and retired early ; her mother feared she was sick, and came up to her room, as she often did, to see that all was right. Sabra tried to speak cheerfully, but her mother knew something was wrong. Sabra said she had the headache, and it was true, for she always had the nervous head-ache after weeping. The next day she was unable to go to the shop. Towards evening, Samuel came to see why Sabra was not at work. His mother told him that she had not sat up any during the day ; he was out

of humor, said he hoped she would give her some medicine to take, so that she might be able to go to the shop
the following day, for everything went wrong when
she was away ; that the girls had done nothing but
waste during her absence ; that they would as soon dry
paint by moonlight as in any other way ; that he had
just found a rack full of articles left out doors to dry
in the rain.   He wished she would go and remain there,
if she was not able to work.   He said her time was
worth a dollar a day every day ; he had rather either
of his men would leave, than her.   He never thought
what he had said to her about the Bible.   After he
had gone, his mother went up to her room, and said,
" Cheer up, you do not know what Samuel says about
you ;" and then related what he had said.   Sabra was
not in humor to rejoice, but merely replied : " I always
endeavor to please him, and to save all I can."   " We
all know that, my child," said her mother. " We know
that you are careful, and that you save all you can, in
everything ; but it pleases me that Samuel thinks so
much of you."

Sabra knew very well that nothing grieved her
mother so much as to have Fred or Samuel speak
wrongfully of her, and she never told her mother
when they reproved her, if she could avoid it.   She
endured all this kind of trouble silently.   She fully realized her situation in the family, as an adopted child,
although she seldom heard any allusion made to it.
She was satisfied that no mother ever loved a child

more ardently than her adopted mother loved her;
and she was always happy when she could please her,
and careful of saying or doing anything that would
injure her feelings.

When she was able, she went to the shop to work.
The girls laughed at her; called her foolish. Henrietta said she would bring some fairy tales there, and
see what he would say to them. When Samuel came
to the shop, he appeared pleased to see her there ;
said he hoped she was better. She replied that she
felt quite well. He went off singing. Henrietta
could scarcely keep from laughing. After he was
gone, she said it was well it was not her, or she would
have given him sauce. Sabra attended teachers'
meetings during the week, and she thought if he would
allow this privilege, she did not care for others.
The fact was, she was becoming well acquainted with
Theodore. She had always desired this, from her
earliest recollections ; when he wore a red morocco
hat, and she a blue jockey. They had seen each
other almost every Sabbath at church, when Sabra
had been at home, and had often met at singing school;
and they each had entertained the same regard for
each other from childhood; and this regard was about
to terminate in an engagement. She knew that
Samuel did not approve of it ; she expected every
day when he would mention the subject, and she
dreaded the consequences ; she thought it was none
of his business, and she prepared herself to tell

him so; she had occasionally seen the fire and smoke, and knew the volcano would eventually burst. He did not approve of her attending evening meetings; it was only for company home. He would say, the girls could not attend to their work as well during the succeeding day, but they did not care for these expressions, as long as he did not forbid it.

After Theodore had visited Sabra more than a year, and probably they were engaged, he took it upon himself to express his disapprobation. Jason and Henrietta were there on a visit. He commenced by saying, that Sabra had gone through the woods, and was like to take up a crooked stick at last! if it was her choice, he did not see as they need care. He thought that Theodore was a steady, industrious young man. " What is he ?" said Samuel; " nothing but a clerk ; no more capable of obtaining a living than either of my apprentices ; besides, he is *poor*, and has not much salary. I tell you, that she is going to throw herself away." Sabra could bear it no longer; she let the volcano burst from her mind ; she told him plainly that it was none of his business, and that he would find that she would do as she pleased. Said she, " I know that he is poor, but I do not care, as he is industrious and temperate. If he would take a glass of liquor now and then, use profane language, like some other, I suppose *you* would think him a fine fellow. I cannot converse with any young man without being reproved by you. It is not long since, while taking a walk, I accepted the hand of a gentleman, to assist me over a small brook, and we walked hand in hand in company with the rest. You saw us, and afterward reproved me severely. Emma did the same, but you said nothing to her. I think it is time for you to let me have my own way. I shall do as I please in this affair, unless some others interfere." Samuel was astonished to hear her talk in this manner. She had always listened silently to his reprovals, until the present time. He said nothing more, but soon went home. Jason said he was glad to hear Sabra talk to him; she had done perfectly right. Her father and mother said they were glad, also, to hear her defend herself; that Samuel always said too much, and was overbearing. Sabra knew she had done wrong to feel angry. She soon retired to her chamber, fell upon her knees and wept bitterly; she prayed fervently that God would forgive her : " Oh, if I were only a Christain, I should never feel angry." Perhaps if she had been chastised for weeping when young, she might have been broken of it ; but no : she had always been petted, and this was all that would cause her to cease. Often would Asenath go to her chamber, and endeavor to cheer her spirits, when she knew Samuel had been reproving her ; but a severe turn of the nervous headache always followed. Experience aftwards taught her better. The bleak winds of adversity often rolled their boisterous waves against her frail bark and, had it not been for Christian fortitude, she would have been wrecked upon the shoals of disappointment,

CHAPTER XXIV.

SABRA DESIRES TO BE A CHRISTIAN, AND OBTAINS A GOOD HOPE THROUGH GRACE.

Sabra's mind became deeply impressed again of the necessity of being a Christian. Professors of religion seemed indifferent and inactive, and she knew not how to take a decided stand. She had heard Rev. Mr. Fillmore preach, and his sermons always left lasting impressions upon her mind. It was seven miles to the church where he was stationed. It was impressed upon her mind that she must go and hear him. She asked her father if she might have the horse, and then asked Joel Parish if he would go with her. We have said before that they had been long acquainted, and the right kind of friendship existed between them. He readily consented. On the way, Sabra conversed much upon the subject of religion. She knew that Joel was inclined to be sceptical, but she knew also that he had a pious mother, and she could talk freely with him upon the subject. They entered the church ; the good man was already there, but he looked unusually solemn. The hymn and prayer were solemn. The text was read in a pathetic manner; it may be found, Zech. 9th chap., 12th verse : " Turn you to the stronghold, ye prisoners of hope ; even to-day do I declare that I will render double unto thee." He said it was possible he might be addressing some who were not prisoners of hope. He illustrated the case by an anecdote which was very affecting; it might apply to those who had often grieved the Holy Spirit, and that it had taken its everlasting flight. Sabra thought perhaps it might apply to her condition, but he proceeded to show that they would have no more sorrow for sin, or desire to become Christians; that they would find no place for repentance. In the afternoon, his subject was the intercession for the barren fig-tree, " spare it this year," &c. While he was preaching, a ray of light burst into her benighted soul; and she formed resolutions, the grace of God assisting her, that she was enabled to keep. She told Joel she was was resolved to be a Christian, let others do as they would. He replied: " If I could hear preaching like that, I might believe there was a reality in religion." Sabra told her father and mother what a good sermon they had heard; and how well Joel liked it. She retired to her chamber early, but not to bed. She took her Bible, and read and prayed, and resolved to spend the whole night in prayer, if she did not obtain mercy. She resolved that, if she perished, she would pray, and perish only there. She found no relief for some time. The adversary told her that she had sinned away the day of grace, and that she need not pray. Darkness, thick darkness filled her soul, but she still cried for mercy. She heard a voice saying, " Though your sins be as scarlet, they shall be white as snow; though they be red like crimson, they shall be as wool." The darkness was all removed; the light shone about her, and she was unspeakably happy. She no longer doubted her acceptance with Christ, and she longed for morning to come, that she might tell to all around what a dear Saviour she had found. There was no one up stairs but herself. She felt as if she had been floating upon the boisterous ocean, upon a frail bark, and just miraculously landed upon the shore ; and could she wait until morning to tell of her miraculous escape ? Yes; she would not disturb them, but she would go to bed, and wait until morning. After some time she fell asleep. She dreamed she was in a beautiful place, where everything was praising God. She joined in singing a favorite hymn ; it awoke her mother, who hastened to see what was the matter. She was singing the last line as her mother opened the door; it awakened her. Her mother inquired what was the matter. She said, " O, mother, I was so happy ; but I was dreaming." " But," said her mother, " you frightened me. I was afraid you were sick." No, mother, but I am very happy."

In the morning she took her breakfast as usual and went to the shop to work. She informed the girls how happy she felt; that she was sure she had experienced a change of heart, for everything appeared lovely. She tried in vain to work; she left off, and said she would go to the house. She was astonished that any person could rest easy who was unconverted; and felt alarmed for them all. As she went out, she met Joel; and informed him how happy she was; that her sins were all forgiven, and then begged of him to neglect religion no longer. She went to the house, and informed her mother of the change wrought in her feel-lings. Her mother said, "You have become a Chris-tian; only be faithful, and you may be the means of doing much good." She spent the day conversing with all whom she met, upon the subject of religion. She asked her father to appoint a prayer-meeting at the house; he did so, and she was very happy in telling to all around what a dear Saviour she had found. There were a number convicted of sin.

One evening, not long after, they were gathered together at her mother's, as they often did, and were going to have some popped corn; they parched it in a long-handled frying pan. Sabra had kindled the fire in the old fire-place in the kitchen. Joel said he would assist her. Sabra commenced the subject of religion; said she would like to be a missionary. Joel said, "If I thought my condemnation would not be a hundred times greater than the heathen, I would be happier than I am at present." "I am rejoiced to hear this," said Sabra; "then you are beginning to see your need of a Saviour. O seek religion now, and you will find mercy." Sabra often conversed, sang and prayed with him. After a few days of deep con-viction, he obtained pardon, and had a good hope of his acceptance with Christ. They both united with the church at the same time.

Sabra thought it the duty of all Christians to make a

public profession of their faith in Christ as their Saviour and unite themselves with the people of God; but she knew not where she could make herself the most useful. She desired that all party spirit should be subdued; and that all Christians might agree. But this was not so. Christians seemed to differ exceedingly in their belief. She finally came to the conclusion, that the Lord made them Christians, of one heart and of one mind; and that discord and party spirit was the work of Satan. She often thought of her pious uncle, and found much of the same spirit among all Christians. Her peace of mind was uninterrupted. There was one place in particular that seemed very beautiful to her; she often resorted thither, to pray God to renew her spiritual strength, and give her grace to enable her to perform the vows she had publicly made.

We will here insert a few lines from her private journal, April 10th, 1831 : " I am sitting under this favorite tree, upon the bank of this lovely river, where I have often been blessed in answer to prayer. O the peace, the joy there is in believing in Christ! My peace is like the gentle stream that rolls before me ; there is not a wave disturbs my peaceful breast. I know that I have a mansion in the skies, and sudden death to me would be sudden glory. I have a conscience void of offence toward God and man, and all is peace within. O that I could find language to fully represent the beauties of religion to others ; but, alas, a finite being cannot fully represent the truth of religion. I must leave this favored bower ; perhaps I shall never be permitted to visit it again.　Joel passes this place when he visits his dear mother.　Will he remember that he has solemnly covenanted to serve God ?　O that God would keep him in the faithful discharge of every duty, and may he sometimes think of me when I am far away !　He seems like a dear brother to me ; but alas !　I must leave him, and all my associates. O if I could but live near, where I could see my friends, how happy I should be !　but I must leave all that is dear to me, and go among strangers.　O that God would prepare me for this great trial, and give me grace to bear all that awaits me in future life !"

CHAPTER XXV.

SAMUEL'S PROJECT TO ESTABLISH HIS BUSINESS IN THE
WEST.—SABRA'S MARRIAGE, AND HER TRIALS.

Soon after Sabra experienced religion, Samuel began to talk of the propriety of Theodore and Sabra being married ; he also formed plans for their future welfare. Sabra felt somewhat disappointed at this, but having always yielded to his opinion previously, she could do nothing else at this time.　They had not thought of marrying at present.　Sabra was contented to remain where she was ; and when she married, she desired to live near her dear mother. But Samuel had different plans ; he thought that if they would go West, and get established in his business, it would be profitable. He had given Jerry Forrester encouragement of assisting him in business, and he was now of age. He proposed that Theodore, Jeremiah, and himself would enter into partnership, find a suitable place on the western borders of New York State, and commence business. Theodore knew nothing of the business, as a workman, but he could learn ; and besides, he had a tact for business, and was a good salesman. Sabra had acquired a thorough knowledge of it; and on account of her knowledge of the business, and her services, they were to share equally, by paying equal capital. Samuel hurried the plans as fast as possible, as soon as he got the consent of the parties. He encouraged Sabra by telling her that he thought he should live there himself some time. At evening she would retire to her room, to gaze upon the gentle moon, which had so often lighted up her quiet room, and think it was the only object upon which she could gaze in future that would appear unchanged. And then, with her heart overwhelmed with grief, she would exclaim to herself : " Why does Samuel wish me to leave my beloved friends and home to go among strangers ? Who will attend him, when he is sick ? Who will take care of dear mother ? and then again, Jason and Henrietta ? Ah, why not let me live where I can see them often ?" After weeping profusely, she would fall upon her knees, and beg for that

G

grace which alone could assist her to bear up under her heavy afflictions. Her nights were spent in wakefulness, and her days in laborious exertions to prepare for her journey. She must work for Samuel as long as possible. Less than a month was given her to prepare for housekeeping, the wedding, &c. She had worked for Samuel nearly three years, and he owed her, for her services, over seventy dollars; she thought that this would furnish her with many useful articles; but what was her surprise to find that this must be turned in as capital, for to make up Theodore's share. Her father said he should stick to his old motto, not to help the children until he had done with his property; then they would have it all; if her mother chose, she might give her a bed, &c. Samuel said he would give her the wedding dress, and that she and Asenath might go to the store and select one for each; they did so; they were the same in quality, but of different color.

Sabra went to make her last visist at Jason's; it was a sorrowful one; she had spent her happiest hours there; there she had a dear brother, and sister, who had always regarded and treated her as such. Jason said he would go with her, and see her settled in her new house; he said the rest of the company might start a week before they did, and select their place of residence, and then they would arrive as soon as necessary. This cheered her exceedingly. He told her that they would have a fine journey on the canal boats; if they arrived in time, they would go and visit their uncle, who lived

in Chautauque county. Samuel intended to establish
his business near Buffalo; this was where they were to
meet. As soon as Sabra returned, she informed her
mother that Jason was going with her, and that they
would not have to start with the rest of the company.
She rejoiced greatly to hear this; and, said, " I can
hear all about your situation when he returns."

Sabra had formed many ideas of the West; some
were very erroneous. She had heard of log houses, of
shanties, &c., but she had never seen dwellings of this
kind. Sabra's exertions to get ready for her journey,
her loss of sleep, her nervous excitement, &c., preyed
upon her system, and her health became impaired.
She had a violent pain in her side, and a severe cough;
but did not complain, lest she should cause her mother
trouble and anxiety; she knew that her mother felt
very sorrowful to have her leave, and that she also feared
she was fast going into a decline, for she had said her
symptoms were alarming.

The wedding-day was fixed, and they invited all the
near relatives of both families. The ceremony was to
be performed by Mr. Sanderson, Theodore's father;
and his twin brother, Thaddeus, and Miss Henry, were
to wait upon the bride and groom; Joel and Jeremiah
assisted in waiting upon the company. Some of the
company were very joyful, while others felt sad.
Sabra endeavored to appear cheerful, but her heart
was filled with sadness. They were all invited to spend

the next day at Mr. Sanderson's. Now, Mr. Sanderson was called an aristocratic gentleman ; he was very
precise in his manner, and there were certain forms
which must be strictly observed in his family ; some of
these forms he wished his son Theodore to adopt and
practice.   He was very particular in giving advice to
the newly-married couple. Mrs. Sanderson seemed
quite pleased with her daughter-in-law; expressed a
great desire that she could live near her.   She also had
many presents for Sabra.   After they had got back
to Mr. Hudson's, Henrietta asked Theodore if they
were alway as precise in every particular incident at
his father's, as they were that day. He said, " It is
nearly the same every day."   She replied, " I am surprised that *you* are not more precise."   Said he, " I
dislike formality."   In a week from that time, Samuel,
Theodore, and Jeremiah were to start upon their
journey.   Sabra's strength failed each day; the day
before they started, she was unable to leave her room.
A physician was called; he said her symptoms were
consumptive ; that perhaps a change of climate and the
journey might improve her health.   Her cough increased, but the medicine he gave her relieved her, and
he thought perhaps she might be able to leave in a
week.   Samuel insisted upon starting; he said Jason
would take good care of Sabra, and that he intended
to establish his business at any rate, and that the
machinery was already shipped, by the way of New
York, and he wanted to meet it ; and he would go,

whether she was able or unable. She was able to be
helped to the window, to see them leave, and she
thought to herself that she was taking a farewell view
of them all. She felt calm and resigned, and that
peace within, which gives perfect reconciliation to the
will of God. She thought, to depart and be with
Christ would be far better; and she thought, also,
that if she died then, she could be buried near her
own dear home, and not among strangers in a strange
land. Well would it have been for her, if her Heavenly Father had been pleased to have taken her to
himself, at that time; but alas! this was but the first
trial of her faith. Asenath was very kind to her, and
endeavored to comfort her, after they were gone; she
remained with her every night. One night Sabra had a
dream that appeared to weigh heavily upon her mind;
she dreamed she started on her journey with Jason,
and arrived at Albany; that she was taken sick, and
unable to rise from her bed; she thought she saw Theodore come into the room; she extended her hand
toward him, and exclaimed, " Oh, Theodore! how
glad I am to see you!" but he came not to take her
hand; he merely looked toward her, and walked out,
without even speaking. She wept aloud, and it awakened her; some time elapsed before she got composed. She related her dream to Asenath, and
said, " Is it possible that Theodore, who has been dear
to me, from my childhood, will ever treat me with
indifference? or is he sick and unable to speak? She

pondered upon the dream until it seemed like a reality. Asenath tried to persuade her not to think of it. As this dream passed from her mind, other trying thoughts rushed in to trouble her aching heart. She would speak of the children, and weep bitterly. There was little Ordelia, Asenath's youngest daughter, whom we have not before mentioned; she was a year old; Sabra had nursed her and her mother when she was an infant; she loved her exceedingly. People said this child was the image of Sabra; she had black eyes, and the expression of them were like hers; perhaps she would never see her again. And there were Fred's children; she loved them all; he had two sons and one daughter; she must leave them all, and her dear father and mother,—all must be left, and she to go, she knew not where.

Notwithstanding all her troubles, she began to amend; the medicine had a good effect, and the next week she became able to start on her journey, accompanied by Jason. The family accompanied her to the town where they were to take the stage coach. Asenath took little Ordelia with her, and she gave the last parting kiss: long did Sabra recollect this last kiss. Her father gave her five dollars after she entered the stage. Sabra endured the fatigue of the journey very well for a few hours, but towards the night the way was rough and mountainous. It was necessary at some of the hills to clog the wheels, to prevent them from going too fast down the hill. Some of the Green

Mountains are frightful to those who cross them in a carriage. Sabra became very tired, and unable to sit up without support. Jason proposed to remain at the next town, but she insisted upon going as far as Greenfield, for she had been told this was half the way to Albany, and the stage stopped there over night. When they arrived there, poor Sabra was as helpless as a child; they carried her into the inn and laid her on a bed. Jason ordered some proper restoratives; she told him she thought her present illness was only fatigue, and in a day or two she would be better; but Jason was much excited, he thought she would never be able to continue her journey. Her cough increased, the pain in her side was severe. She requested Jason to get a mustard poultice for her side, as that had often relieved her of pain. The landlady said Pulmonary Balsam would be good for her cough. As soon as convenient, he ordered a bottle; she found it a great benefit. The next afternoon she was able to be up and walk about the house. As soon as they thought proper, they pursued their journey towards Albany. There were no plank roads at that time, but a few miles near Albany the road was macadamized; this was a curiosity to Sabra; she had heard of such roads, but never seen one. She knew they would have to cross the Hudson river before entering Albany, and she felt quite anxious to know how. Jason told her the boat was rowed by horse-power. This alarmed her; but he explained it satisfactorily to her. She supposed they would leave the stage before entering the boat, but they drove upon what she supposed was a bridge, and then stopped. Sabra clung to Jason, quite alarmed; she thought the bridge must be floating, for she felt it rock. They soon calmed her fears, by telling her that they had driven the stage coach upon the boat, and that they crossed the river in this manner every day.

It was between sundown and dark when they entered the city. Sabra was fatigued and disheartened; she thought Albany a lonesome place. When they arrived at the public house, she was still more disgusted; they found it crowded, and the rooms filthy. They had expected to have remained there until Sabra became invigorated, but it was so unlike their public houses in Massachusetts, that they devised means to leave as soon as possible. Had they been directed to other parts of the city, they might have found a good house, and have been well entertained. After tea, Jason went out in pursuit of a canal boat, to take them to Buffalo. It happened that it was not far to the office of the Merchants' Line; he found a boat that would leave the following day. Sabra felt homesick and disheartened; she could scarcely speak without a tear. Jason tried to comfort her; he informed her that " the captain appeared to be a very pleasant man; had but a few passengers; that the journey would be easy; that he could leave the boat often, and get whatever she required; that the captain and himself were going to hunt wild game along the banks of the canal ; he says he often takes his gun and leaves the boat, and goes on shore to hunt ; he knew where to find plenty of game." Jason had taken his gun on purpose to hunt wild game in the West ; he hoped to kill a deer, and he had heard his uncle say there were plenty.

Sabra had a poor night's rest ; she thought of home. It seemed far, far away, and still she was not half way to her journey's end ; indeed, she did not know where her journey would end. The next day they went on board the boat. She found a small apartment for ladies at the end of the gentlemen's cabin, or the dining-room, or sitting-room —she knew not which it was called, for it was used for all these purposes. There was, however, a display of neatness and order which she did not expect to find. She went into the ladies' room; it was unoccupied; there were beds piled on either side, one pile just high enough to lounge upon. Jason and the captain prepared for her a place to rest comfortably, and left her. She then wept freely, and prayed earnestly that God would give her strength to perform her duty, and grace to bear her troubles. At night she found that the seats around the cabin were boxes filled with beds; they were taken out, and swung one above another, three in height. They were not very soft, but they fixed an extra one for Sabra. She thought of what she had heard of people sleeping upon the soft side of a plank, and supposed it must be like the beds they had there. The first night there was one only, and the cook or the cabin maid occupied the room with Sabra. She was very kind and obliging.

The next day Jason and the captain went on shore and killed some birds, which they had dressed, and had cooked for her. Sometimes they caught fish and cooked them for her. The captain persuaded her to try porter, to strengthen her; she consented, and thought it increased her appetite. Jason had bought a quantity of Pulmonary Balsam in Greenfield. She continued to take this for her cough. Her health improved every day. By the time they reached Buffalo she had nearly recovered. She loved to journey on the canal boat ; they had good company, and evenings they would sing upon the deck. Sabra thought it sounded beautifully upon the water. She had many a good sing while upon the boat, and many a happy hour she passed while sitting upon the deck, conversing with Jason upon the beauties of the scenery ; and while admiring the works of the Supreme Being] in nature, her very soul was drawn upward to nature's God, from whom she thought emanated every particle of goodness. Mr. Cameron and his sister had accompanied them nearly all their journey. They were going to reside near Buffalo. Sabra became quite attached to them. They had journeyed together more than a week, and had promised to visit each other as soon as they got settled.

When they reached Buffalo, they found that they were to be disappointed. Jason found a letter direct ing them to go back immediately to Rochester ; also stating that Samuel had gone down the Lake to Kingston, Canada West; that he thought of locating there. This intelligence grieved Sabra extremely; she could not visit her uncle ; she was sorry to leave those with whom she had journeyed; and, worst of all, perhaps she must go to Canada. She had been accustomed, from her earliest recollections, to hear Canada spoken of unfavorably. Erroneous ideas had been instilled into her mind. She thought upon it, and she was indignant. She murmured because they had not informed her that they thought of settling in Canada, and said she would never have started from home to have gone there. She finally said, if they went there without consulting her upon the subject, they might go alone, and she would go back with Jason. Here she displayed her wilfulness, for she afterwards found good people in Canada, and became attached to the place. Jason tried to quiet her, but she was determined in her own way, and he assured her that she might go back, if Samuel would not settle in the States. They returned to Rochester. They arrived there the day Colonel Rochester was buried, and attended his funeral. They had never attended so large a funeral, or seen so much honor displayed upon such an occasion. During the day they met with Theodore and Jerry, who were watching for them. They were very happy to meet. Samuel had not returned, but they were to remain there until he came. They had an opportunity of seeing the

Genesee Falls, and many other curiosities. Sabra was passionately fond of admiring and gazing upon the beauties of nature. A heart like hers could never be unhappy while attracted by the goodness and greatness of that Being whom she loved to worship and adore.

At length Samuel returned. They were happy to hear that he had selected a place in the town of O., upon the eastern bank of the St. Lawrence River; it was a lovely place, and fills the stranger immediately with admiration. They were to start from this port as soon as possible. Samuel had become acquainted with an aged gentleman by the name of Judson; and, by earnest solicitation, he had consented to board them all, until they could find a house suitable for their family. This engagement was favorable to Sabra. Their family at this time consisted of three persons—Mr. and Mrs. Judson, and their only daughter, of sixteen years. They had two sons, who boarded elsewhere.

Mrs. Judson was a kind, motherly woman. Sabra esteemed her highly. Through the remaining part of this narrative, we may often speak of the kindness of this family, and of the friendship that existed between these two families. Mr. Judson informed them that, a few days previous, the house next to his residence was vacant; they might have obtained that. Sabra thought if they had hired that house, she would have been perfectly contented. Jason informed Samuel that he would find a house while the rest of the company were fitting up the machinery in the shop. He then told Sabra to rest easy, for he would have that house. He went to the man that occupied it to make inquiries respecting the house. He said he had just bought it; if he had not moved into it, he would rent it. Jason offered to pay him well for moving, and he consented. It pleased all of them exceedingly.

In less than a week they were comfortably situated in the next house. Sabra was cheerful, and did all she could to make her brothers enjoy themselves while they remained with them. Samuel had some business transaction with Deacon Varson; he told the deacon that Theodore was a minister's son, and a member of the church : that his sister was a good singer, had lately experienced religion, and would be a useful member in the church ; she was a good singer, and had been a great assistance to the choir. The deacon called upon them, and appeared quite friendly. Through his instrumentality they united with the same church to which he belonged. This conclusion pleased Samuel, who often had conversation with the rich deacon. He informed the deacon that his sister was a fine girl ; finally said he : " she was only brought up as an adopted daughter, in my father's family." This, of course, made him appear of a little more consequence. Sabra did not know, at that time, that he had taken pains to say this to the deacon. They got their business started, and then were preparing to leave. Mr. Judson said to them that he would be a father to their sister, and that she might always feel at home in his house. This was very kind, and it rejoiced Jason greatly ; he said it would be cheering to his mother to hear of their kindness. We will here remark that Mr. Judson always kept his promise ; a father could not have treated her more kindly.

The day they were to leave, Samuel spoke to Sabra upon the subject of religion. He told her that his mind was deeply impressed with his need of a Saviour ; that he did not leave her alone without a Saviour, and . no hope. She endeavored to tell him how to become a Christian. She felt happy to hear him express his feelings, and made it a subject of prayer, after he was gone. He told her that he should miss her if he should be sick. Poor man ! he did not think of another who would miss her more, and whose grey hairs would go in sorrow to the grave. Alas ! that the love of gain should ever blind a child to the welfare of an indulgent parent. Sorrow often encompasses the tomb of parent and child, when this is the case. That others may not do the lic !

It was a solemn time for all of them when they parted with Jason and Samuel. After they were gone, Sabra retired to her room to weep and pray ; fervently did she entreat her Saviour that he would convert her brothers, and grant her grace to bear her afflictions, and strength to perform her resolutions, in regard to her family devotions. She told Theodore that she had enlisted in the cause of Christ for life ; that she intended to attend all the appointments of the Church, and that family prayers, both night and morning, must be attended at the commencement. He thought it would be a great cross, but she reminded him of his father's last request. At night, when they came in, Sabra got the Bible and read a chapter, and Theodore was enabled to bear the cross, and an altar was erected, around which many afterwards were blessed. Instead of one prayer being offered alone, as a duty, three or four were often offered alone, as a privilege. How sweet is the incense of prayer around the family altar, and particularly when every member of the family performs this duty! How choice are the blessings they received! none but those who have received these blessings can comprehend them.

After they united with the church, they were invited into the choir, and soon began to feel at home. Deacon Varson always attended meeting; he was the leader of the prayer meetings, and an exemplary Christian. He stood, indeed, like a pillar in the centre of that church: he was the chief support, both spiritually and temporally, and he stands there at the present day; and may the Lord still spare him for his usefulness, and may he live to see, like Simeon of old, the salvation of God come to that people; he has long prayed for it.

CHAPTER XXVI.

SOME OF THE TRIALS ENDURED BY SABRA WHILE
PERFORMING HER DOMESTIC DUTIES, AND HAVING
THE CARE OF THE SHOP.

Sabra endured trials and hardships, during the two
succeeding years, which could not be described.   She
seldom found time to retire to rest until midnight, and
arose before the sun, in the morning.   Those who
are accustomed to the western part of New York State
know that a few years ago, before sidewalks were made,
the roads were almost impassable after a rain, on
account of the depth of mud.   Often when Sabra was
going to and from the shop, which was half a mile distant, she found, when she raised one foot after the other
that it was minus the rubber; she would stand upon
one foot, and extricate the rubber from the mud, and
place it upon her foot.   She often thought if that was
the road to wealth, she had rather dispense with riches;
but Samuel had placed her there, and she must perform
her duty, and answer for the services of another; but
alas! for her, she found it the road to poverty, instead
of wealth.   Had it not been for the kindness of Mrs.
Judson, and her daughter Mary Ann, she would have
been discouraged.   During the three first months they
all passed through severe trials; having but a small
capital, and being among strangers, before they received
any income from their business, their money was all

exhausted. Deacon Varson and Mr. Judson had already kindly helped them in emergencies, and they did not like to apply to them again. Their flour and meal were gone, and, in fact, they needed much at the time. Theodore had tried at several groceries to get flour, &c., but had not succeeded. He was quite discouraged; and wished himself back in Massachusetts. He was not accustomed to trouble like this; and knew not what course to pursue.

When Mr. Warren made Sabra the present before alluded to, he desired her to keep the money on interest until she went to keeping house, and then buy some valuable pieces of furniture, that she could keep, in remembrance of the family. She had the money still in her trunk, with the interest it had accumulated; she intended to buy with it a clock and a mirror. Should she make the sacrifice? She thought a moment, and got it and gave it to Theodore, saying: " Do not be discouraged; the Lord will provide." He was quite surprised; he knew not that she had it by her. He said, as many other men would say, that she might have given it to them before. However, it relieved their present embarrassments, and they were not cornered again so closely.

Mr. Judson often reminded Sabra of his promise to her brothers, to watch over her as a father; and he often told her that she ought not to work so hard; that she ought not to attend evening meetings. She told him that it refreshed her; that if she remained at

H

home, she would have to work. He said he was going to write and tell them how she toiled, night and day; for she was ruining her constitution. She begged him not to write, on her mother's account; she did not wish to have her know that her work was laborious.

CHAPTER XXVII.

SAMUEL AND HIS WIFE UNITE WITH THE CHURCH, AND WRITE TO SABRA.

About three months after Samuel returned, he wrote Sabra a letter. It commenced with the endearing appellation of "Dear Sister." What a thrill of joy animated Sabra's heart when she read this; and Asenath had written and addressed her the same. They were both feasting upon the first-fruits of pardoning love. They were happy, and wished to make others the same. O "sweet messenger of peace," why dost thou not always remain in the heart of the new convert! They wrote also, that Fred and Marina were converted, and other members of the family; there was a great revival in that neighborhood; that they often spoke of her, and wished her there. This letter cheered Sabra exceedingly, and gave her renewed strength to perform her Christian duties.

CHAPTER XXVIII.

JEREMIAH FORRESTER IS HOPEFULLY CONVERTED, AND UNITES WITH THE CHURCH.

The church where they worshipped at that time, only had preaching once in two weeks. Their minister lived about thirty miles distant. He became acquainted with Mr. Sanderson's family, and often spent the night with them. This was a great help to them in their religious devotion.

The ensuing winter, they had a protracted meeting. Jerry's mind was often exercised upon the subject, but he had never experienced religion. Sabra thought this would be a favorable time to urge him to seek forgiveness. Earnestly did she pray that the Holy Spirit might convict him of sin, and that he might be brought to the knowledge of the truth. The prayers of God's people were answered, and many were converted. Jerry was one of the number united with the church, and was a useful member. Their family worship was often like a little prayer-meeting, where each member unites in the service.

CHAPTER XXIX.

SAMUEL SENDS THEM A JOURNEYMAN.

Samuel thought they needed assistance in the shop, and he sent them John Barnard. Sabra felt quite annoyed at this, for he was a man of dissipated habits, and she detested the use of spirituous liquors. He was a clever fellow, only when he chose to have a spree ; and these he would have occasionally ; but he usually stayed away from the house until he became sober. At one time he had been drinking intoxicating liquor, and went to the shop sick. Theodore and Jerry tried to get him to go to the house, but he said he could not see Sabra. They came in and told her his excuse. She prepared some nourishment for him, and went to the shop herself, and persuaded him to take it, and go to the house. The change of climate and unnecessary exposure brought on the bilious intermittent fever, so prevalent in that region, and he was very sick ; his physician considered him dangerous. Sabra attended him day and night. She had a bed placed near for Theodore, that he might assist her, if necessary. John would often say to Sabra, " I shall never reward you for your kindness." She would reply : " If you will reform and become a Christian, I will feel doubly repaid." She endeavored to warn him of his lost condition, while under condemnation ; of the willingness of Christ to save all who sought him. He became alarmed, and viewed himself a sinner, and earnestly desired salvation. Often, in the stillness of the night, would Sabra kneel, and pray fervently in his behalf. He faithfully promised, if God spared his life, that it should be devoted to His service. He did not obtain an evidence of his forgiveness, until some time after his recovery; but he continued carefully to study the word of God, and was seldom seen seated without his Bible in his hand. In a few weeks he obtained an evidence of his acceptance with Christ, and was very happy. Often in the prayer-meeting would he speak of the goodness of God, and faithfully would he warn others to turn to Christ. He remained happy while he resided with them, and when he left he was rejoicing in the hope of Heaven.

Sabra always attended all the prayer-meetings of the church, unless sickness prevented. They had a female Missionary meeting, and at the choice of official members, she was chosen president of the society. She remonstrated against it; she felt unworthy and unqualified; but the minister's wife did not reside in the place, and the deacon's wife belonged to another church, and she was obliged to accept the office. She remained in that office until she left the place, and probably would have given good satisfaction, had it not been that Brother and Sister Burdensome moved into the place, and joined the church by letter. He possessed some peculiarities, which soon placed him in the possession of deaconship; and as long as he remained a mechanic, he performed his duty pretty well; but when he assumed the position of a merchant, his religion became an outside show, and his heart was evidently corrupt. His wife partook of the same spirit; she was fearful that some member of the church, that labored for a living, would wear a garment made of the same material like her own. " Such a sister was a useful member, but, however !" and there was always a " but, however," or some other appellation like the former attached to a certain class of members. She was never burdened on account of her own sins, but she groaned under the burden and weight of the sins of other professors of religion. The deaconship seemed to rest on her shoulders. Sabra often suffered on account of her venemous tongue, but she bore it patiently.

Sister Burdensome was astonished that Sabra should take such care of Mr. Barnard, if he had a watcher ; she would get up to give him his medicine, and she had often been seen up at one o'clock. " I tell you, Sister C., this ought not so to be ; there is something wrong there in that family ; and then, if Mr. Sanderson is gone, or detained at home, she comes to meeting with Jeremiah. These things ought to be looked after. O if church members would only live exemplary lives, religion might prosper," and then she would draw a deep sigh. Sister C. replied : " I think Sabra tries to live the life of a Christian. She has many duties to perform ; and has a class in the Sabbath-school ; she always attends that, and the prayer-meeting ; she commenced from a sense of duty ; and never talks of the faults of others. I think you must be mistaken, for I am well acquainted with her, and I think her motives are good." " Well," says Sister B., " I hope so. You must not think I meant to say anything against Sabra, for I despise tattling or evil speaking." Sabra would always hear of her remarks, but she choose to suffer wrong rather than do wrong. She could not see why it was necessary for her to suffer this way, but she found that it was for the trial of her faith, for she always repaired to the throne of grace for support, and she found her strength renewed. In every towering fabric of falsehood, and the severest trials of her life, Sabra has always had occasion to say : " It was not an enemy that reproached me, else I could have borne it ; but it was mine equal." Oh, how deep is the wound when inflicted by a friend! it seems liks a poisonous venom that cannot be healed. Nothing but the grace of God can repair an injury done by a friend or brother.

Sabra's labors around the sick bed were not at an end when John recovered. Jerry was taken with the same fever. Patiently did she watch by his bedside. She recollected the last advice of her kind mother; it was this : for her to be kind to Jerry, and treat him like a brother; to remember that he would feel lonely. He had lived in the Hudson family a number of years : they all liked him ; he was kind and obliging, and was always ready to grant Sabra a favor, or to assist in doing services about the house. She had no one now to see that the pail was filled with water, or the box with wood. She knew that the tongue of the slanderer, which no one can tame, was already set on fire by the powers of darkness; but she feared not; God was her helper; she would try to perform her duty. She watched by his bedside with all the solicitude of a sister. Before he recovered, Theodore was taken sick. This was a still greater affliction. She then thought if God would preserve her health, she would not complain. She could attend upon him without restraint.

Who can describe the depth of feeling, or the tender solicitude of the affectionate wife, as she administers to the wants of him she loves, while she feels that she is stronger than the arm upon which she has relied for protection? How earnestly will she pray for his recovery, and watch for the first flattering symptom! He was not as sick as the other members of the family; the fever had passed off lightly, leaving him afflicted with boils.

They employed the services of Urana Hunter, who lived with them two succeeding years. Her father and mother were both members of church; they had brought up thirteen children; all of them were members of the same church. Urana would often tell Sabra what Sister Burdensome had to say concerning her and others. She would tell her to keep her news to herself; but she would reply that it was too good to keep. She knew not that it grieved Sabra, for she seldom made any reply, but listened silently.

CHAPTER XXX.

SABRA VISITS THE HOME OF HER CHILDHOOD.

It was decided before they left home, that if nothing happened to prevent, Sabra should visit them at the expiration of two years, accompanied by Jeremiah, who would have business there at that time. Sabra was preparing for the journey, and she had many unpleasant thoughts intermixed with her fond anticipations. Her heart was filled with ecstasies of joy, when she thought of seeing her dear father and mother. On the other hand, she must leave Theodore at home, and undoubtedly Sister Burdensome would groan and sigh as usual, and consider it improper for a member of the church to go a journey unaccompanied by her husband; it would be a topic of conversation during her absence.

After laboring during the day, and being fatigued, she retired to bed late in the evening. Sabra felt very sad, and could not refrain from weeping. Theodore inquired the cause of her sorrow. She informed him. He replied: "I suppose people will make remarks if you go; perhaps you had better remain. You have no father or mother to visit." He was unaware of the effect this sentence would have upon Sabra's mind, for he had not alluded to her adoption since their marriage; she had not heard it mentioned for years, and it had never before grieved her as at the present time; at this time it caused the tears to flow more freely. Could it be possible that Theodore had uttered this unkind remark ? She uttered not a word. A daughter never loved a mother more tenderly than Sabra loved her mother, and that affection was mutual. Had it not been for this strong attachment, means would never have been devised to have her removed to such a distance. Many have attempted to describe the painful emotions of the wounded heart; but our language is not competent for this. That heart which is capable of intense enjoyment, is also susceptible of the greatest suffering. It was some days before she regained her usual cheerfulness. Sabra had carefully put away all her wearing apparel, that it might receive no injury in her absence, and had given Urana many charges respecting the fire, &c. She was a careful housekeeper, and always attended to her domestic affairs closely.

The day arrived that they were to leave. Theodore and Mr. and Mrs. Judson accompanied them to the boat. Sabra felt sad when she left, but she soon thought she was on the way to see her dear mother, whom she knew was expecting her. They had always kept up a correspondence. Her mother's letters were full of kindness. After a long journey upon the same old canal, they arrived at Albany, and then took the stage to Worcester. They arrived at home safely, and enjoyed a happy meeting. All things appeared as usual about the house, and what was best of all, they all appeared glad to see them. The children had grown larger, but the number was the same.

After a few days, Sabra went to Jason's. She could enjoy freedom in conversation here. If she spoke of her trials, she knew her mother would not know of them. O how delightful it is to unburden the mind to a faithful friend! The sad heart often becomes joyful by sympathy. She had not unburdened her mind with as much freedom for a long time. " Oh," said she, " If I could only live where I could come and see you often, how happy I should be !" Her visit must not be long in any place, and she returned. Jason and Henrietta said they would visit her at their father's, before she went home.

Sabra was informed by her mother that she had a present of a hundred dollars for her; it being a part of the property which she received at her mother's death. Samuel had advised her to give it to her at this time. Sabra thought it rather strange that he should encourage this; but, alas! she knew not the depth of calculation which governs the business man. She was quite pleased, and told her mother how it would relieve her embarrassments; that she could have many things which she required; she had not a single drawer, or closet, and not enough common dishes to keep house comfortably; she could now have pans and bowls, &c., and not be compelled to empty one dish into another, as she formerly had done whenever she wished to use one. She also was informed that Jeremiah was to be married, and take his wife home with them. She would have company; that would be pleasant. Jerry was to receive some money from his father's estate, and put it into the company; this would add to his capital. Samuel suggested the propriety of Sabra's giving her money to Theodore, that he might not be left in the rear. Sabra made no reply, for her mother was present; but when she retired, her pillow was wet with tears. She wished she had been brought up as a servant, then she could have had more independence. She felt that she had been a willing slave, and was always like to be one. She felt that the crosses and trials which she daily experienced were more than she could bear. She wished she could see Jason; and she told her mother that she had better keep the money, that she did not want it. Mrs. Hudson did not see through her son's designs as clearly as Sabra saw them. She got Samuel to count the money, and gave it to her, telling her she hoped she would use it as she thought proper.

They had already remained longer than they intended. They started back, but were detained on their journey by the irregularity of the boats, and did not arrive at home as soon as expected. Sabra had written two letters, but the last one had miscarried. Sister Burdensome said it was just as she expected; she did not believe they ever intended to come back, for Sabra had not left any of her clothing about, not even an old shoe, for Theodore to look at. She had

even told Theodore what she thought, and endeavored
to sympathize with him. Sabra had not informed them
of Jeremiah's marriage, for she wished to surprise them
on their return. They were kept in fearful suspense
about a week, constantly performing the hardest kind
of drudgery for the evil one. You may judge their
surprise when they saw Jerry, accompanied by his wife.
Urana told Sabra the slang that was going the rounds,
but she chose not to notice it; she thought they would
feel rather chagrined this time; and she performed
her duties as usual.

When Theodore knew that Jerry had got his money,
he lamented that he had not the same amount. His
credit was established, and a friend had kindly offered
him all the capital he required, but he was always
afraid of getting in debt. Sabra also feared that; she
had rather deprive herself of any article than to owe
for it. She brought forth the hundred dollars, and
asked him if that would answer his purpose. She told
him that a lawyer, who was a friend of theirs, had
accompanied them on the boat, and that she had told
him how they were situated in business, and that he had
advised her to give the money to him, for the company;
and for him to convey it to Jason, in trust for her,
in case any accident should occur to the company.
Theodore was pleased with this proprosal, and gladly
secured that share of the machinery which belonged to
himself, to Jason, for it had all been purchased with
her money. Mr. G. drew the writings, and all was

right.   Sabra felt quite contented, and they seemed to prosper in their business; but Jerry, or his wife, was neither of them contented.   She did not like the West, nor the manners of the people.   Jerry proposed to sell out to Theodore.   He made the offer, and Theodore accepted, and paid him his demand; and at the expiration of one year they moved back.

During the time they remained, they all lived together in unity.   They esteemed each other as sisters and brothers.   At one time Sabra was very sick, and not expected to live.   Mrs. Forrester was very kind to her. When told that she could not live long, unless some favorable symptom appeared, Sabra calmly asked Mrs. Hudson if she thought that day would end her sufferings.   She desired Theodore to tell her mother that death had no terrors; that she longed to depart; she knew her sins were forgiven, and could view by faith the land of rest, where she would be free from sufferings, and be permitted to praise God forever for his goodness.   But God, for wise and unknown purposes, spared her life, and she began slowly to amend.

When conversing with a faithful minister, she inquired why she could not always feel that calm resignation which she felt when she viewed death so near.   He replied, that our Heavenly Father knew the grace we required; that He gave the Christian dying grace when death approached, and living grace while living, and conquering our enemies.   These words were as nails fastened in a sure place; and, often, when doubting for lack of faith, they would cheer her drooping spirit.

Sabra felt very lonesome after Jerry and Louisa left. She did not wish to return; she thought they had passed through their greatest difficulties, and that their worldly prospects were favorable. She knew they owed no person, unless it was Samuel, and his account could not be much. They knew that he was prospering rapidly in his business; he had sent them word that he had given fifty dollars at one time to the Missionary Society. Surely a man in his circumstances, possessing a generous heart like his, would not wrong them. They had many friends. Mr. and Mrs. Judson and their family seemed like near relatives. Their sons were often at home, and Mary Ann often visited a number of days with Sabra. All holidays they were invited home, as Mr. Judson would say; and truly, no place seemed so much like home to Sabra; if she wished for counsel and assistance, she went to Mrs. Judson. Sister Burdensome said such friendship might last a short time, but it would not last long. She wondered that Sabra did not choose to visit more among the church members where they belonged. We are happy to say, that the same friendly feeling existed as long as life endured, and probably will be re-animated in another world. The same friendly feeling exists at the present day by the surviving members of the families.

CHAPTER XXXI.

SAMUEL AND HIS WIFE VISIT O.—HE IS DISSATISFIED
WITH THE PROSPECTS OF BUSINESS, AND ADVISES
THEODORE TO RETURN.

Soon after Jerry and Louisa returned home, Samuel
and his wife started for O. They arrived safely.
Sabra was rejoiced to see them. She loved them with
all the tenderness of a sister; but, alas! she knew not
the object of their visit. Samuel soon made it known.
He said he did not know about Jerry's selling out so
easily; if he could not get all his share, he should hold him
responsible with Theodore. Theodore did not know
that Samuel had as large a bill against the company.
Samuel advised Theodore to close up the business
as soon as possible, and go back to Massachusetts,
and try some other business. This was even worse to
Sabra than leaving home at first. She was now comfortably situated, and she knew it would be a long time
before she could be as well off. She must pass through
the same trials again. She remonstrated against it,
but in vain. Samuel said, it was no use; it would
take all the machinery, at the price he was willing to
give for it, to pay him. He said they must sell everything that they could dispose of, for it would not pay
to carry it back; the machinery he could use, and he
would take it at some price towards his pay. No
person can imagine Sabra's disappointment. After

Samuel started back, they began to dispose of their furniture and collect their dues. At the next covenant meeting of the church, Sabra's heart was full of grief; she fully realized that she must leave the place where she loved to worship God; she must leave the church, her class in the Sabbath-school, and must leave the choir, where she loved to sing God's praise. They asked for a letter from the church; it was unanimously given. She returned home, and spent the evening in prayer and communion with God.

Two or three days after, there was a sick man brought to their house; they had known him in Massachusetts, and he had been at their house before in O)r Mr. Smythers was taken sick upon the boat, and knowing their hospitality, desired to be carried to their house. He was destitute of money, and among strangers. Every thing possible was done to arrest the disease. A skilful physician was called, who attended him faithfully. He expressed his opinion that it was doubtful if he ever recovered; that he had the typhoid fever; that it had been settled some days. " But," said the kind doctor, " we will do all we can for him." His mind was impaired, and he was already partially delirious. The doctor said to Sabra : " You understand taking care of the sick, and he will have ths best of care; perhaps he may recover." Sabra's heart was full of trouble; situated as she was, how could she perform the task ? She knew he had no relatives to apply to for assistance. It appeared

I

that God designed her to perform this duty, and to Him alone she must look for strength. She thought of the remarks that were made when she had attended upon others, but they had ceased. She concluded that she would do all she could. She watched him night and day. She often felt wearied and exhausted. The doctor said it was too much for any person in her situation; that she must have assistance, or she would be sick herself. He said he would send watchers: but she must see that he took all his medicine, for much depended upon that; and he was often obstinate and unwilling to take it, and would not take it from others. The doctor had seen this often, and knew that no person else could make him take it; consequently, if he had watchers she must be called to give his medicine. The second week, another fever set in, and he was delirious. Little hopes remained of his recovery. The fourth week he began to amend; and the fifth he was able to sit up. The young men kindly offered to assist him, when he became able to be moved, and provided for him a place to board. Sabra could now leave him at intervals. Mary Ann was there; Sabra asked her if she knew of a woman she could employ to wash for her. Mary Ann said: "Take your bonnet and come with me to the grove. I will find you a woman that will assist you." She did so; and they were soon at the door. Mary Ann rapped: a good looking woman, well dressed, opened the door, bade them walk in and be seated. Sabra felt abashed.

The woman thought she had seen Sabra before but knew not where. She immediately called her Mrs. Sanderson, and began to invoke blessings to rest upon her. Sabra delivered her message, and she replied, " God bless yer, Mrs. Sanderson, I will come to yer, if it is on my hands and knees. It was yerself that saved me and me children from starving, when we first landed here in Ameriky; and wasn't our money all gone ? and wasn't all of us sick ? and yer gave us herbs that cured us, yer did ; and yerself and Mrs. Taylor, gave our children clothes, and made them dacent to go to school. May God bless yerself and Mrs. Taylor, and long life to yer." By this time they were all three weeping. Sabra had forgotten the circumstance, but her referring to it, brought it fresh to her memory. She recollected a family who took lodging for a few days with a family who lived in the next house; that she had been told they were destitute and sick; she had called to see them, and give them such things as she thought they required. She had often given them vegetables from her garden, and meat to boil with them. Two years had passed since this occurred; besides, this was a usual occurrence with her, for the poor were never sent empty away: if she had but little, she would divide; and if called upon to visit or watch with the sick, she never refused. This incident had entirely passed from her mind, like many other duties which she had performed for the needy. At this time she felt fully recompensed for all she had ever done. Her heart was filled afresh with love to God, who always rewards the cheerful giver. The next morning, when they arose, they found Mrs. Mc. sitting upon their door step. She was doubly rewarded for that day's labour. Being about to leave, Sabra found many useful articles, which she laid aside for her.

CHAPTER XXXII.

SISTER BURDENSOME AND SISTER PRECISE CALL UPON SABRA UPON SPECIAL BUSINESS.

While attending to her washing and upon the sick, she was interrupted by a call from Sister Burdensome and Sister Precise. She invited them, politely, to be seated. They inquired after Mr. Smythers. She invited them to go to his room. They had not called before during his sickness. They declined, saying that they called upon special business. They hoped she would not think hard of them. They said that some of the sisters of the church were dissatisfied with her conduct of late, and had solicited them to call upon her and converse with her; perhaps she would make acknowledgments that would be satisfactory. She inquired what their accusations were. They replied, that she had been seen up at a late hour; and that too, when Mr. Smythers had watchers. They had also been told that she would arise and give him his medicine, and many other services which were not unnecessary. Sabra replied; "The doctor has been very particular to have him take all his medicine, and often he will not take it from any person except myself. I feel perfectly justifiable in what I have done for him. If that is all, I have no acknowledgments to make; I need your sympathy rather than reproof, for my trials are great." Sister Burdensome drew a sigh, and said it was a pity ! She thought that such kindnesses as she had shown to Mr. Smythers, and him a stranger, belonging to the poorer class of society, was unbecoming to a professor of religion ; we should extend our sympathies to the brethren and sisters of the church. They arose and left the house, saying that she would be waited upon again.

Sabra retired alone, to weep and pray. She could not understand why it was her heart was filled with joy on one day, and that the next day she must drink the bitterest dregs of disappointment. She was soon called by the sick man ; she could not be absent long without being called ; and hastened as soon as possible to his bedside. Said Smythers, " What is the matter ? You have been crying ; you are tired, I know. Why did you not let me die ? If it had not been for the kindness of you and the good doctor, I should not have been alive now to trouble you !" Sabra replied, that it was the mercy of God alone that preserved his life ; that he might have time and space for repentance. The kind physician was the only one who seemed to sympathize with Sabra in regard to her great trials. He had many patients at the time, and was often very tired himself ; sometimes he would sit a few minutes to rest.

That day Sabra related to him the object of Sister Burdensome's call. He thought it ridiculous. " But," said he, " I would not notice it; she is always troubled about somebody. She sometimes prays for me in public. If it were not for hypocrites like her and some others, religion would prosper better in this place."

Thus did poor Sabra receive one trial after another, which she never could have borne, had she not been blessed with the sustaining grace of God. Alas! how sad it is that inexperienced youth, who are possessed of virtuous hearts, should be forever under the searching eyes of those monsters, in human shape, who are always lurking about, peaking into key-holes, or half-curtained windows, that they may spoil the fair reputation of others, to get material to build their own characters upon. They are cannibals whose appetites are as insatiable as death. It is more strange, that when the virtuous are caught in their net, the world looks coolly on. The thief is pursued with avidity, and brought to justice; but the slanderer is allowed to walk upon our carpets, lounge on our sofas, and sit at our tables. We should beware of volunteer witnesses, who are ever ready to drag their neighbors before the tribunal of public opinion. We should be slow to condemn; it may be our turn next. The whisper may have already commenced which may swell into a deafening noise, and be repeated from neighbor to neighbor, and from town to town, until an indelible blot be stamped upon the fair page of our reputation. It is no light, trifling affair to believe a lie, if it is told by a professor of religion, or an eminent member of the church. The heart once wounded by the piercing arrow of defamation, never heals; innocence may have been proved, and the false witness condemned, but the memory of that one deep wrong will never be eradicated; it will glide silently like a ghost among all future joys.

The injured one may rise to affluence and influence, but the scar still recalls the injury to mind; and too often its woof is visible in the premature winding-sheet, and its victim finds peace in an early grave; but its record is in Heaven, written by the pen of the Almighty, and he will avenge the innocent, and punish the slanderer.

CHAPTER XXXIII.

MR SMYTHERS IS REMOVED, AND MR. AND MRS. SANDERSON RETURN TO MASSACHUSETTS.

The young men of O. kindly obtained a boarding-place for Mr. Smythers. As soon as he became able, he was removed thither, where he received kind attention until he recovered. Mr. or Mrs. Sanderson never received any remuneration for their trouble, although he often promised, during his sickness, that he would recompense them, if he recovered. They had previously disposed of most of their furniture; they packed the remainder of their bedding, &c. They left the village and the society that was dear, very dear to

Sabra.   Many friends accompanied them to the boat;
Sabra took her leave of them with a sorrowful heart.
They arrived in Massachusetts safely.   Her father
and mother welcomed them back.   The machinery had
arrived at Boston by shipping.   Samuel knew that
Theodore's share had been intrusted to Jason, for
Sabra's benefit, but he thought he had a right to claim
it all.   Beside all this, he had a demand on Theodore
of two hundred and fifty dollars.   Theodore thought
Sabra had better give up all freely, or Samuel would
have hard thoughts of them, and that would grieve her
mother.   When she saw Jason, she told him she was
going to let Samuel have all that had been secured to
her.   He said she was very foolish; but she made the
sacrifice, and all was gone, and Theodore gave his note
for the balance.

Thus they toiled hard four years, to find themselves
nearly three hundred dollars in debt, beside what they
had accumulated the three years previous to their
marriage, together with all Sabra's presents, which
amounted to two hundred dollars more.   The business
man thinks not of woman's rights; no, not he! no more
than those men who legislate our laws.   Some of them
do not allow a woman her hard earnings, that she may
clothe and feed her children.   Her husband may be a
drunkard, or a gambler, and the articles she has toiled
day and night to obtain, may be sold by the sheriff to
pay his bill.   Talk of freedom! where will you find
slavery like this?   We are happy to say that in some

places, laws like this have been eradicated, and woman
is protected, and enjoys the privilege of eating her
own bread, using her own furniture, paying her own
debts, clothing and educating her children; and woman,
poor, feeble woman, has the pleasure of bringing up
her children to be ornaments in society. It should be
so everywhere. Ye men who legislate, hasten the
time when women may enjoy that for which they have
toiled night and day to procure, and that for which
their mother's have toiled unceasingly to lay by for
them; your poor-houses would not contain the number
they now do, and your penitentiaries would be less
crowded; your insane hospitals have less inmates.
How often has the poor, industrious mother, who was
blest with intellect, industry, and economy, and capable of bringing up and educating her children, been
driven from her home, and her own earning been
snatched from her, to pay the debts owed, perhaps, to
the liquor seller, or the gambler, or some other transaction by which she or her children never received a
farthing. She becomes disheartened and discouraged;
she gives way to her troubles, and at length becomes
a maniac. Her children are cast upon the charities of
an unfriendly world; they grow up without an education, or the cultivation of morality; and tell, if you
can, where this unhallowed influence will end? Ah! a
finite being cannot trace the end of this legal transaction; eternity alone can measure the abyss of woe into
which multitudes have been plunged, who might have

been brought up by their mothers, and been ornaments to society, and able to sustain their parents in the decline of life, and thus reward them for their kindnesses. Countless ages alone can answer this, for its influence may continue beyond our comprehensions.

Had Sabra enjoyed this protection, herself or her children would never have been destitute of the comforts, or even the luxuries of life, for God always blessed her undertakings, and crowned her labors with success. She soon went to Jason's. They all received her kindly. She saw at once that Fred was not pleased to see them return; she did not like to stay at her father's on that account, although her father and mother urged it. Theodore wished her to stay in the country, until he found a permanent situation in the city; his health was failing; he was troubled with the dyspepsia; and he had already obtained the situation of a clerk in a large establishment in Boston. Sabra wished to have a room, and keep house; her situation required it. Jason said she might have a part of his house. This pleased her exceedingly; but her mother had persuaded Theodore to leave her with her a few months. She used all the arguments she could to remain at Jason's; told him that it was eighteen miles nearer Boston; that he could visit her oftener; but he was always sure that his judgment was the best, and urged that it was her duty to submit willingly. Sabra always had submitted willingly, but at this time she submitted reluctantly. She could not bear the idea of being a burden; she was unable to earn money as she formerly had done. They were entirely destitute of money, and she needed many things. She remained a few weeks at Jason's, and then returned to her mother's. After Theodore had gone to the city, she went to, a friend, who was soon to be married, and disposed of some articles which she could spare, and obtained money to answer her present emergencies. Samuel and Asenath were very kind to her during the time she was at her father's. They were always ready to bestow on her a favor; would often ask her to ride with them. Fred said nothing against her staying there; but actions often speak louder than words. At evening, she would retire to her room, and write in her journal, or to some friend. She often wrote to Mary Ann Judson; they corresponded as long as they were separate. She spent many happy hours in solitude. She was in the house where God first spoke her sins forgiven, and took all her guilt away, and the place was dear to her; the memory of those happy hours often filled her soul with peace. On the Sabbath, after they were all gone to church, she would take her Bible and hymn book, read a chapter, then engage in prayer, afterwards sing God's praise, which was her delight. She constantly enjoyed peace of mind. The greater her afflictions were, the nearer would she approach the throne of grace. She loved to take her album, and read verses that were penned by her Sabbath-school scholars; and pieces written by other friends often cheered her drooping heart.

In the month of February, she gave birth to a daughter. There was great rejoicing at this event. She was impatient to see Theodore, that he might receive the prize. As soon as he received the intelligence, he hastened home to rejoice with the rest. Sabra deeply felt the responsibility of being a mother. She desired Theodore to get a tenement as soon as possible, that the family might be together; but she passed through many trials before he succeeded; when he did, she was very happy to be by herself again.

After they moved to Boston, Sabra had more time for improvement. She felt her need of general information, and appropriated a portion of her time each day to reading, which became a great benefit to her. She regretted that she had not .acquired a better education, and devised plans to accomplish this. She reviewed her childhood studies, and made great progress; she studied Walker's Dictionary, and was astonished at her ignorance of the meaning of many words. Theodore's father was a college educated man, and he commended Sabra for the course she was taking. He kindly gave her books, which were very useful to her. Sabra could not enjoy this privilege long; she seemed destined to changes. Theodore's health became more impaired. The bleak east winds did not benefit his constitution; and being confined in the store, without bodily exercise, his disease became more established. His twin brother, Thaddeus, was in New York city, in business; he wrote him that, if he was there, he could get him a situation any day. Theodore was always hasty in his decision, and made up his mind immediately to go to New York. He acquainted Sabra with his intention as soon as he went to the house ; said he could go to the country and get a tenement for her, and she must move there until he got established in New York, when he would send for her. She begged to stay where she was, but he said it would be more expensive; and his mind was always made up without consulting her, and there was no changing it afterwards, for he was set in his opinion. He went to her father's, and informed them of his intentions, and procured a tenement for Sabra about a mile from them. There was a widow lived in the house he engaged, and she was very kind to Sabra and little Helen ; she did not like to live alone, and they lived happily together, Sabra urged Theodore to take what little funds they had, for she was fearful that he would not get business immediately. Thus she was left again, without money or means, expecting Theodore would send her money as soon as he found employment ; but judge her surprise and grief upon receiving his first letter; for it informed her that ere she received it, her husband would be on his way to one of the Southern States.

Theodore had met with a merchant from Alabama, who was purchasing goods, and was desirous of obtaining a clerk or foreman. He made Theodore a liberal offer, and would pay all his travelling expenses. He accepted this offer, and started, in company with the merchant, for the Southern clime. He was flattered to believe that a change of climate and of diet would improve his health. His letter was full of tender regret that he could not see his wife and child before his departure; but it was impossible. This letter seemed to Sabra more than she could bear. She now fully realized that she was left alone, and that she must devise means for the support of herself and child; she immediately sought employment with her needle. Helen was two years old. Samuel often employed her when he was hurried in his business. He soon proposed that she might have a part of the tenement he occupied, and board those who were employed in the shop. She went to her father Sanderson for advice. He had moved from the place where he had so long labored, and lived sixteen miles distant. He thought she had better accept Samuel's offer. She began to prepare to move, but her heart was sad, for she loved to be alone. Mrs. A. regretted to have her leave, for they lived very happily together. She prospered very well in her new situation. Samuel and Asenath were very kind to her. Her father and mother were glad to have her near; and often did her fond mother regret that she could not live in the family with them. Her father was willing, but, alas! he feared Fred.

Joel was one of Sabra's family; there had always existed a true friendship between them. True friendship exists only where God himself prepares the ground. They often conversed together upon the subject of religion, and the time when they first made a profession of their faith in Christ; they both belonged to the same church; a brotherly and sisterly feeling always existed between them.

Sabra toiled very hard; but what of that? she could earn her own living. She often worked until a late hour, but she could have the satisfaction of knowing that she was laying by something every week for the day of adversity or for future enjoyment. Her father's health began to decline, and she was unable to labor, except some light work. He loved to have little Helen with him; she would often go and take her breakfast with them; they were pleased to have her, and would set a plate for her. Sabra usually took breakfast early, before Helen was up. It annoyed Fred to have Helen go there to take her breakfast, and he began to reprimand his father and mother and Sabra, for allowing it. Sabra kept her away for some days. Her father inquired the cause of her absence, and persuaded her to let her come, as usual; said there was no person but they two, and it was lonesome; that he enjoyed his breakfast much better when she was present, for she was very talkative. He told her not to mind what Fred said, but let her come, as usual.

Every few days there was something for Fred to scold about; there was always something wrong in Sabra. At length he hit upon the right plan; he knew his father was tenacious of keeping the farm in the hands of his own posterity, and he was the only one who wished to labor upon it, and he thought to leave his father in his old age, or even to say that this was his intention, would accomplish his design. He even carried his design so far as to go abroad to look for land. He said there was no use of staying there : they could not all be supported by the income of that farm. His father felt quite sad ; and knew not what course to take. He told his wife and Sabra that he would rather live in a secluded place upon his farm, called Thorny-Gutter, in a hut, than to hear Fred forever grumbling ; he felt quite sure that his days were nearly finished, and he wished to see his children all united. Sabra told him that Samuel talked of sending the men to a shop in the adjoining town, where there was a large water power ; if he did, she would go to board them, and then Fred would not grumble about her being there. This proved to be a fact. The water failed at home, and he gave up entirely. Soon after, Sabra moved ; her family was not large as it had been, and she found time to work at one part of the business herself ; and often she earned a dollar per day.

About a year and a half after Theodore went South, he sent Sabra money. Previous to this, she had paid Samuel the interest upon the note he held against them. She could not endure the thought of being in debt, and it often disturbed her peace. She now thought she could cancel the debt, and get the note. She collected what she had earned ; and that, with what

Theodore had sent her, was sufficient to pay the whole amount. She carried it to Samuel, but to her surprise, he refused to take it. He kindly told her that he should never take it from her. She thought him very kind in this transaction, but still she was troubled about the note.

She often heard from Theodore ; his health was grad- ually failing. Sometimes he was unable to attend his business ; but he said nothing of returning back. More than two years had already passed since he left, and, many a lonesome day she had passed, yet she enjoyed religion and a firm hope of Heaven. A longer time than usual had elapsed since she had received any letter from Theodore. Suspicion, that foe to all happiness, which is often worse than reality, had filled her mind with trouble. She thought he must be dead, or he would write to her. She wrote, and wrote again, but received no answer.

One afternoon, while Sabra was at a female meeting, at a near neighbor's, she was called home. She met Theodore's father at the door; his countenance was sad. She was filled with fearful emotion, but he led her to the room. There lay Theodore upon the lounge ; he was a mere skeleton, scarcely able to reach home. His father told Sabra that he feared Theodore had relaxed in the performance of his religious duties, but she must continue as usual to have family prayers, and be faithful in conversation with him. He remained with them until the next day, and then returned home.

K

Poor little Helen could not be persuaded to think that the strange sick man was her papa. She would say that her papa looked like Uncle Thaddeus, and that this man was not like him. She was an affectionate child; if she saw her mother weeping, she would say, " What is the matter, mamma? I will be good." Little innocent creature; she never realized the loss of her father. That evening Sabra read a portion of Scripture, as usual, and asked Theodore to lead in prayer, but he declined, and requested Joel to pray. She prayed and others followed; it was like a little prayer-meeting. She often conversed with him upon the subject of religion. He told her frankly that he had not walked with the church since he left Boston; the reason why was this : He had seen so many professors of religion, who could make long prayers, whom he thought were immoral and dishonest; he had lost the enjoyment himself and was almost persuaded to live in universal salvation, through the merits of Christ. She asked him if he did not believe that he experienced a change of heart before he made a profession of religion. He admitted this, and acknowledged the enjoyment he then possessed. She endeavored to explain to him that the improper conduct of professors of religion would never confound the doctrines of the cross, or the reality of experimental religion; that there were hypocrites among the professed followers of Christ, while he was with them upon the earth, and that undoubtedly, they were as numerous at the present

day; that if one in every twelve were all that would
be thrust out at last, as not having on the wedding
garment, it would be a small portion, compared to
what might be lost by believing false doctrines ; and
awful in the extreme would be the portion of those
who knew their Master's will, and did it not. He
soon saw his error, and had a great desire to again
enjoy the blessings of forgiveness, and peace with
God. This he obtained, and was desirous of again
uniting with the church, where he first belonged, and
where Joel and Sabra then were members. He then
was able to ride, and they went to the church, and he
was welcomed back. It was sacrament day; it was
a solemn time, long remembered by many. He was
just able to sit during the service, and then rested at a
friend's, where he formerly had lived. They remained
two days in the neighborhood where he had spent his
youthful days, and saw many of his old associates for
the last time. They then went to Sabra's father's,
where he enjoyed his last visit. He was cheerful
and happy ; he only lamented that he had not walked
in the path of duty, and thereby served God more
faithfully.

After they had returned home, and he had rested,
he began to talk of their worldly prospects. He had
laid by a small amount of money, notwithstanding his
ill health. He could pay Samuel, and have a small
sum left. Sabra told him that she had offered to pay
Samuel, and that he refused to take it from her.

Theodore rejoiced greatly to hear this; said that they freely gave up every cent they possessed to him, when they returned from the West, and perhaps Samuel thought that was sufficient. "Surely," said he, "if he would not take it when you offered it to him, he will not take it now, when he sees me upon the brink of the grave, and you to be left a widow, and our only child fatherless. But I will offer to pay it, and thereby get the note, that you need not fret about his holding it against you." He was surprised to find how economically Sabra had managed; that she had all the funds he had sent for her use, upon interest, besides a small amount which she had earned herself; she also had a good supply of clothing. Thaddeus had given her a splendid silk dress, and a valuable shawl. Jason and Henrietta had also given her clothing. Little Helen had received many presents. Now, if Samuel should refuse to take the two hundred and fifty or sixty dollars, which he had laid by for him, and give up the note, he could leave his family in comfortable circumstances. He knew that Samuel could boast of his thousands of dollars, and that he would never feel the loss of it. He knew, also, that it rightfully belonged to Sabra; that it had been lawfully secured to her; that she had freely given up to him more than that amount. His hopes were brilliant; but alas! why should disappointment take the place of hope, and thus sadden the heart of the disconsolate!

CHAPTER XXXIV.

SAMUEL VISITS THEM—TAKES HIS MONEY, AND CARRIES IT AWAY.

Samuel had removed from the homestead, and resided eleven miles distant. He had built himself a splendid cottage, and was doing an extensive business, in company with a rich man. The fortunate spoke in his wheel of fortune was upward; indeed it seemed stationary. He was a stockholder in the bank, and prospered in all his undertakings.

A few days after the conversation alluded to in our last chapter he called to see Theodore. Asenath and little Ordelia were with him. Theodore did not tell Samuel what Sabra had communicated to him about the note, but during their conversation he told him he could pay him, if he wished for his money; that he had been as prudent as possible, and had saved a little of his salary, although he had always poor health, Samuel said he supposed it would be as well to have it settled now; that he was in want of money, and immediately produced the note. Theodore had laid by the amount in gold and silver coin; he counted out both principal and remaining interest; it was quite bulky. Samuel tied it up in his pocket handkerchief. He did not stay to tea, but seemed in a great hurry, and soon left. Sabra's heart was full of grief. When they were getting into the buggy, she turned away; her eyes were full of tears. She went to the window; saw him reach the money to Asenath. She felt sure they were

carrying away that which rightfully belonged to the
fatherless and widow. Ordelia said to her papa :
" What makes Aunt Sabra feel so bad ? she is crying."
Asenath said, " Theodore looks very bad ; he will not
live many days."   " Yes," said Samuel, " he looks
bad ; worse than I expected ; he'll not live long.   I
went in just the right time.   It increases my credit in
the bank to have money deposited there.   The business
man needs all the money he can get, to carry on business successfully, Sabra can manage well enough without this."   "I feel sorry for her," said Asenath ; " she
looks feeble and exhausted ; she has not had a whole
night's rest since Theodore returned back."   " I suppose not," said Samuel ; " but then she can bear more
than any person I know of ; she will work, you know,
if she can find anything to do."   They were going to
spend the night at his father's.   They drove up to the
door ; his mother went to the buggy with a joyful heart,
for she was always glad to see her children and grand-
children.   Samuel reached her the money, saying,
" Take this, and take care of it."   " What is it ?"
said she ; " it is heavy for a small parcel."   Little
Ordelia said : "Grandma, that is all money : papa got it
from Uncle Theodore, and you don't know how pale
and sick he looks ; and aunt Sabra was crying when
we came away."   Mrs. Hudson took the money, and
drew one of her long, deep sighs.   Joy had fled from
her cheerful heart, and sadder thoughts were occupy-
ing her mind.   She knew that Samuel had refused to
take the money from Sabra, and she thought he would

never take it; she knew that Sabra had freely given up to him all that had been secured to her, and her heart was sad; but thought that at some future time, she would recompense her for the sacrifice she had made; but, alas! she knew not how easily others would rule her affairs by foul stratagem.

The next day, Samuel returned home, carrying his treasure. He went to his office. His partner was there, busily engaged looking over the books. He said: "How did you succeed with Sanderson?" "O very well. Sanderson is a clever fellow; and you know I am not easily duped; I did not intend to lose that; I have lost enough already. A business man needs all the money he can get. I mean to look out for one, and that is myself." "But I thought you would give that to Sabra; she needs it." "Not I. She has a faculty of taking care of herself; she is young. If she needs help, I can assist her in the future. Sanderson is almost gone; poor fellow! he has not long to live." He lit his cigar, and went out to gaze upon his extensive possessions. Each of these men possessed their own thoughts. The honest man thought of Sabra, as he had seen her before her marriage, in the gay assembly; she then appeared cheerful and happy, with a heart buoyant with hope. He thought of the contrast; a gloom had settled upon her countenance, although she tried to appear cheerful. He knew that she toiled hard, and had already broken her constitution; but, amidst numerous cares, the thoughts of Sabra passed from his mind.

CHAPTER XXXV.

THEODORE'S DEATH AND BURIAL.

Soon after this, Theodore was confined to his room. He became entirely reconciled to his situation. He conversed with all his friends, and those who called to see him, upon the necessity of being prepared for death. Jason came to see them, and brought Hatty to assist Sabra; this was a great relief to her. One day, Mr. and Mrs. Hudson were there. Theodore said : " Father, you have always been kind to me and my family; I thank you for this ; I shall soon leave them ; I hope you will still be kind to them. I am going home first, but you will soon follow. We shall soon both be in eternity ; where we shall meet, and be free from trouble." The old gentleman was much affected ; he seemed fully to realize how short his own life appeared. This was indeed the last time they met on earth. Theodore spoke cheerfully about his funeral services ; expressed his wish that his funeral might be at the church where he first experienced religion, and where he had recently re-united with the people of God, and spoke also of the place where he desired to be buried.

The scenes of the death-bed have often been described, but faintly are they pictured to the human mind. They can better be portrayed in the minds of those who have witnessed the scene : and who has not stood beside the dying ? who has not lost a friend ? We will leave this scene to the imagination of the reader, when we have said, that he passed away, as if sinking in a sweet slumber, leaving his friends to weep for their loss, which was his gain.

The funeral services were attended at the church where he had requested, and according to his wishes; it was solemn scene, long remembered by all present. The funeral services of the wife of their family physician were attended the same hour, at the same place. It is seldom that we see two corpses in a church at same hour. Two of his brothers returned home with Sabra. Kendrick, his youngest brother, was her favorite. He was then preparing for the ministry; she always had applied to him for counsel, in her husband's absence. She felt now that she needed counsel more than ever. She told Kendrick that she knew not what course to pursue; she feared, if she remained where she was, that the voice of the calumniator would be active against her; she feared their attacks more than the actual pursuit of a highway robber. She had already suffered sufficiently by the remarks of the slanderer to know their direful consequences. Kendrick advised her to remain, and follow the same employment; she could earn four or five dollars per week. She told him if she could prepare herself for a primary school teacher, she would like that; then she could teach little Helen herself. He encouraged her in this project; said if she could stay at her father's during the fall and winter, she might apply herself wholly to her books, and be able to commence in the spring; that he would assist her.   She told him frankly that Fred did not wish to have her there.   He was surprised; said he thought a perfect union existed in the family.   Sabra seldom spoke of her trials.   He left her to decide for herself.

Soon after this she went to her father's and asked for advice.   They said she had better remain where she was; that she would be happier there, for she would hear no grumbling.   Her father was failing gradually. Said he, "I have not long to live; perhaps they would like to have you come and live with your mother when I am gone; she will be lonesome, and need some person for company.   I wish to live in peace with Fred the few remaining days I have to stay; my trials will soon be ended.   I have left your mother," said he, " abundantly able to have all things managed according to her own wishes.   I have made my will differently from what I once intended; I have left it for her to manage as she thinks proper.   She is to have one-third of all property to dispose of as she pleases."   Sabra said she hoped he would not be troubled on her account, for she could take care of herself; that she had rather have his approbation than all his property.   Said he, " I hope you will be prospered, and continue to have good courage."   Sabra went home fully persuaded to add all she possibly could to her small stock of knowledge.

After she had retired to her room, wearied with a hard

day's work, she would commit a long lesson, or read some encouragement from the Boston Olive Branch. Who can read that paper without thinking they were created for a high and noble purpose? And we ask who can read the writings of M. A. Denison, and others, who write for that valuable paper, without growing wiser and better? Often, when nearly discouraged, would Sabra find in the writings of Coleworthy something to stimulate her to action. Upward and onward seemed to be his motto, and she adopted the same course.

She wrote a letter to Mr. Judsons family informing them of Theodore's death, and soon received an answer, urging her to visit them. Mary Ann was married, but boarded with her father. She said that her father's health was failing; that he was anxious to see her before his death. Sabra fully resolved to go there in the spring.

One evening, after Mrs. Hudson had retired to rest, she had a wonderful vision, or a magnificent view of the glory of God. She saw a great white throne, and the glorious purity and perfection of the Deity that sat thereon was too pure for her imagination. She seemed to shrink back from the presence of that holy Being, but it still appeared in view. She was invited to join the number of that innumerable company which surrounded the throne, clothed in spotless purity She wished to communicate what she had seen to her children; and invited them all home for that purpose.

She endeavored to describe what she had seen to them, but it was evident that it was past description. She was deeply impressed with the thought that nothing impure or unholy could ever enter that happy place. She endeavored to impress upon their minds that, without purity of heart and purpose, no person could ever enter into the presence of God. Fred said that it was nothing but a dream; that she was always seeing something wonderful. Sabra was astonished to hear him speak lightly of it. After the other members of the family had gone, Jason, Henrietta and Sabra were delighted to hear her speak freely of what she had seen, and to hear her talk of Heaven. She described it as a vision, she had not been asleep. Sabra told her mother that this was intended to disperse her fears; that now she ought to enjoy the hope of the Christian. Mr. Hudson delighted to meditate and speak of this event, and her mind became prepared for greater trials.

CHAPTER XXXVI.

THE DEATH OF MR. HUDSON.

Mr. Hudson's impressions respecting the brevity of his life were correct. He failed gradually; in the month of January he died. Sabra sent for her brother Kendrick, to accompany her to the funeral. He came; the roads were filled with snow, and the weather was extremely cold. They drove up to the door of her

dear mother. It appeared that no preparation had
been made; about the door the snow was lying in piles.
Upon entering the house, they found only one person
within. Sabra nearly fainted; after she was restored
she was told that her father was not buried; that Fred
had insisted upon having the corpse taken up to the
other house : that her mother did not wish to have the
corpse removed, but Fred said there would be more
room there. She was told that her mother had just
gone, and that it was nearly time for the service to
commence. She went into the room wher she had
taken the parting hand of her dear father, only a few
days before, and knelt down and prayed God to give
her grace to bear this affliction, and that God would
sustain her dear mother; she knew that her afflictions
were multiplied. O how she wished that she could
stay with her, and comfort and console her. She knew
well that the removal of the corpse was to influence his
mother to go there to reside. The stratagems of the
designing are artful and cunningly devised. They
walked to the other house. Great care had been taken
to have the snow cleared away around where Fred
lived. Kendrick said : "Is it not singular to have
the corpse removed before going to church ? I never
heard of an instance like this." Sabra made no reply,
but little Helen said : " Mamma, did grandpa die up to
Uncle Fred's ?" " No dear." They entered just as the
mourners were taking their seats. Sabra had but a few
moments' conversation with her mother, for Kendrick

had to return to W. that day. She told her that she would come and see her in two or three days. On their way home, Kendrick asked Sabra what could be the object of having the funeral at Fred's. He said her mother would feel worse to go back to the house than she would be if she had gone directly from it. She told him that Fred said there would be more room. " Oh, fie!" said Kendrick; " the other house would hold twice the number there were present." Sabra had never made any remarks to Kendrick about Fred. She seldom mentioned him to any person. After Kendrick had gone, and she had retired to her room, she felt inconsolable. " Ah!" thought she, " how miserable must those persons be who are bereft of friends and never pray;" for it was in prayer to God that she found relief. According to her promise, Sabra went to see her mother. She found her calmer than she expected, and at her own house. A friend was staying with her for company. Sabra told her that she would come and live with her at any time, if she desired it. She replied that it would be her choice, but that it would be impossible, for Jason had proposed it, but Fred opposed it; he said she might as well move into the house with him first as last; that she would have to. Jason's health was poor; she had proposed to have have him come and live with her, but nothing could be done satisfactorily unless she went there. Samuel did not like to hurt his mother's feelings but he could go to Mrs. Heulet, and get her advise his mother not to have Sabra come there to live. Sabra told her mother that if she did not go to live with her, if she was willing, she thought of going West in the spring ; that she must adopt some means of supporting herself and little Helen. Her mother spoke of the will; said she had not seen it, and did not expect to, for Fred had it ; that he was executor. She said her father had given but little to Jason, or to her, but had left a good portion for herself, to give to whom she pleased, and that she should attend to it. Sabra said it was not property she cared for; it was to have her happy and comfortable. Her mother said, if it could be possible, she would like to have Jason or her live with her ; if not she would choose Samuel next, but she was afraid that she must submit to live with Fred. Sabra went home and applied herself more faithfully to her books. She succeeded in every study but arithmetic : this often puzzled her. She kept her plan a secret. Joel was very kind to her, and would carry her to see her mother as often as she desired. She told him that she intended to go West in the spring, but he supposed she was going on a visit.

A few days after the funeral of her father, Sabra received a kind letter from Kendrick. Rich gifts are acceptable to the poor and destitute, but what gift can compare with sympathy to the sensitive heart. How often she read over and over again Kendrick's letter. You here have the letter, as penned by the kind writer ;

" DEAR SISTER SABRA,—I suppose you may be a little anxious to learn how I got home, after leaving your place last Thursday, and I improve the first leisure hour to write you. I rode warm and comfortable, without stopping to warm; I had a pleasant sleigh ride except in narrow places. The drifts are abominable in narrow roads. I was obliged to get out and tread down the snow in some places. Enough of this: however, I think your curiosity must be sufficiently satisfied as to my ride. I told you that I wrote to father, informing him of the death of your father. I received a reply a day or two since. He was surprised to hear that one of his tried and faithful friends had gone, and seemed to feel deeply the loss. Do not grieve too much, sister Sabra, for your father's departure. I know he was dear, very dear to you: but remember we have a common Father, who is much more watchful and tender than our earthly parents, as He is more able and ready to grant us the favors we desire ; and think, too, that we ought to be grateful to Him for showing such kindness to the friends whom we most love, as to take them, before us, to their happy home, to His parental bosom; and fear not that you will be left friendless when you see those most beloved leaving you, one after another. Be willing, at least, ever to regard me as a brother, in whom you can confide ; and feel that you are a sister in our common family. I had hardly a moment to talk with you, Sabra, when I was at L. I shall, however, next vacation, I think, see you again. Our term closes three weeks from next Wednesday ; I shall expect a long letter from you before that time. You must pardon me, dear sister, if I am too light and trifling, for it is my nature. The religion of Jesus, I can't believe, was ever intended to restrict our cheerfulness. If I am too lively, however, do tell me of it, and I will try to correct myself. I do desire, if I know my own heart, to devote myself wholly to the service of my Saviour, and to make all I do tend to His glory. I believe the same desire fills your soul. Let us pray for each other.

" My respects to your family, and forget not a budget of love to little Helen. Good-by for the present.

" Your ever affectionate brother,

" KENDRICK SANDERSON.

" Mrs. Sabra Sanderson."

———

Sabra went to the trunk that contained her old letters, to lay this one carefully by. She saw a package of letters that Theodore had received while at the South ; she thought she would read some of them. The first one she opened was from her brother Samuel. She was surprised to find that it contained sentences she could not understand. He spoke of the money that was due him ; said Sabra had received some intelligence from him respecting it, but could not tell what it was ; conveying the idea to Theodore that Sabra treated his letters indifferently. At the close of the letter was the following sentence :

" P. S.—Particularly. Should you have anything

L

to write me alone, you can send me a line in a few days
after the first.   S. H."

———

If ever a person desired to converse with the dead,
Sabra did, at this time. Her next impulses were that
she would go directly to Samuel, and ask him what he
meant. After she had prayed for sustaining grace, she
resolved to say nothing about it, but try to overlook it.
" Ah !" thought she, " is this from the pen of him over
whom I have watched in sickness so many long, long
nights, and wiped from his brow what was then supposed to be the cold sweat of death !" Even Fred had
chided her for her attention to him in sickness ; and
now he was misrepresenting her best motives to her
nearest friend on earth. Theodore had never sent any
message to be given to Samuel. He merely said that
he hoped he should be able to pay him sometime. Sabra
had freely offered to pay him, from the pittance accumulated by herself, and the small sum received from
Theodore for the support of herself and little daughter.
She did not wonder that Theodore came nigh stumbling
over the faults of those professing Christianity ; she
felt sure that a cloak of professed Christianity would
prove but a thin veil to cover base corruption like this.
She was more fully resolved to seek her maintenance
among strangers.   One link alone still bound her to
her native home,—her dear mother and her early associates.

CHAPTER XXXVII.

SABRA VISITS HER FRIENDS IN THE WEST.

Dreary winter soon passed away, and lovely spring ushered in. In the month of May, Sabra was ready to start on her journey ; her mother thought it would improve her health. She had moved into the house with Fred,. but had secured the privilege of keeping her dairy at the other house ; she said it afforded her pleasure to go there to take care of it. Sabra was visiting her for the last time before starting on her journey ; she requested Sabra to go and ask Mrs. Heulet if she would take her to Esq. Haskin's on the following day ; Said she, " I am going to get him to make my will." Mrs. Heulet consented ; and Sabra afterwards heard that they went, and that the will was executed. She left her mother in good spirits, promising to write often.

She started from the town of L. in the stage-coach ; the railroad was not then completed. At Albany she took the canal boat, and travelled through the same place she had four times previously passed. Some of the villages were improved in appearance. Little Helen was delighted with travelling. She arrived at Mr. Judson's at night; they received her cordially. Mary Ann (now Mrs. Gleason) appeared less changed than the rest ; she had a noble little boy two years younger than Helen. Their eldest son lived in the village, and was still unmarried; he often called there : it

appeared to her that there had been less changes there
than in other places ; it seemed like home. She was
told that Sister Burdensome still lived there, as busy
as ever; but Sabra cared not for her ; she had not the
guilty conscience to annoy or frighten her. She was
anxious to see Mr. Gleason, but he was away on business. She soon found that Mrs. Judson's health was
not good, and Mrs. Gleason was not then able to assist
her. Sabra endeavored to make herself useful ; she
did not mention her intentions for some time, but
visited among her old friends.

Sidney Judson accompanied Sabra to the church to
a prayer meeting one evening. Brother Burdensome
was there ; he led the meeting ; he seemed to be in
great distress for the prosperity of the church. He
was about to leave them, for a few days, to go to New
York to purchase goods. One would have supposed,
by his prayer, that the burden of the whole church
rested upon his shoulders, and that he expected they
would backslide if he was absent. On their way home,
Sidney asked Sabra if she thought him sincere. She
replied, that she hoped so. He replied, that he did not
believe him, and to remember his word, that he would
prove as great a hypocrite as ever entered the church.
And truly, not many years after, Brother Burdensome
left the church, his family and his creditors, and has
not returned. Sister Burdensome had business of her
own during the summer that engrossed her attention ;
she became more willing to let other people alone. She

knew, by experience, that it was pleasant to have a friend sit by her bedside, in sickness, and brush away the flies, and after she became able to ride, to bring the carriage to the door, and give her a morning drive. Her husband was busy; it was not convenient for him to leave; there could be no remarks made, for her attendant belonged to the same church ; and, beside all this, she was a deacon's wife.

CHAPTER XXXVIII.

SABRA'S SECOND MARRIAGE.

During the summer, Sabra became acquainted with a gentleman of pleasing manners; who possessed a free, open, and generous heart; he was well informed, and very entertaining in conversation. He made no pretension of possessing religion; but in his childhood he had received religious instruction, which had left a lasting impression upon his mind. His parents were professors of religion. Sabra spent many pleasant hours in his company ; they often met undesignedly, and he often called at Mr. Judson's. The result of their acquaintance was, that he made her a proposal of marriage.

Sabra had just received a letter from her dear mother. It was full of tenderness. She addressed her as her only dear daughter. Herbert read the letter, and said she must have one of the best of mothers to write like that. She told him that she was only an adopted daughter ; that she knew no difference ; that she had been taught by her adopted parents never to mention it, but that it was her duty to speak of it now, for perhaps it might be an objection to the proposition just made. He replied, that it was herself that he wished for a companion. See told him that her religious sentiments were firm and deeply rooted ; that she could not sacrifice any of her religious privileges to please any person. He told her that he should wish her to enjoy them, and that he would endeavor not to retard her in the Christian course. She then told him that she must see her mother, and ask her consent; before she gave him an answer. She went home in September, arranged her business, and consulted her mother ; she thought she would be more free from annoyance at a distance, and perhaps she would return with her the next time she came to her native home.

Before Sabra returned, Fred gave her twenty-five dollars, and said that his father had left that for her in his will. He had a receipt ready for her to sign in full, as having received all her portion from her father's estate. She refused to sign it ; said she would sign in full, as having received that amount as a legacy. She told him he might keep the money ; that she could do without it. He handed it back to her, and she signed a receipt according to her proposal. She returned, and married Herbert, but did not give up the idea of teaching. She pursued her studies as usual ; she thought she could more easily instruct Helen by teaching others at the same time. But, alas! how often was she called to drink of the bitter cup of affliction.

Soon after her marriage, she was called to part with her dear, beloved child. God saw fit to take her to Himself; it seemed like giving up a part of herself; she felt that Helen was her all, and she was her earthly idol; she often felt sure that she loved her too well, but how could she help it; she was a lovely child; every person loved her. But soon, in this affliction, Sabra recognized the hand of her Heavenly Father, and she submitted with Christian fortitude. How much easier it is for the Christian to submit to the positive will of God, than when the affliction arises from the persecuting influence of men and evil!

During the succeeding summer, she was alone much of the time, and found time to devote herself to her studies. She informed a clergyman, with whom she had long been acquainted, of her intentions; she told him that she had long felt it her duty to instruct the youth. He kindly offered to assist her; he told her that he would soon make fractions as easy and plain to her as A B C. She soon became as familiar with arithmetic as other studies.

CHAPTER XXXIX.

THE DEATH OF MR. JUDSON.

One great source of enjoyment still remained. Sabra lived near Mr. and Mrs. Judson, and spent many

happy hours with them and their family. But Mr.
Judson's health gradually failed,and he became unable
to leave his room. Herbert and Sabra had often
watched with him, and he talked freely to Sabra about
dying; told her he esteemed her as one of his
own family. One day he sent for her to come and
see him ; she went immediately. Said he, " I have a
particular request for you to perform." He spoke of
forty acres of land which he owned and had cultivated ;
he had been accustomed to ride out to it every day,
in some seasons of the year. Sabra had often been
with him, and admired the location of it ; it was only
two miles from the village, and beautiful land upon
either side of the road. The urgent request which he
desired of her, was for her to accept a deed of it. She
told him that she could not possibly accept it ; that she
valued the existing friendship of his family more highly
than property. He urged his request, by saying that
Mrs. Judson would like to remain with her a part of the
time, and that she would feel more at home if she
accepted the farm. Sabra said that Mrs. Judson would
always be welcome to a home with her, whenever she
choose to remain there ; that the favors they had already
conferred upon her would entitle her to that. She
begged of him not to bestow any of the property upon
her, but let her retain the same position in his family
which she had for many years enjoyed.

After the family circle, she asked them if Mr. Judson's mind was not wandering. They said that he was

perfectly sensible; that he had been quite anxious all day to see her. She did not tell them the conversation that had passed. They supposed it was the subject of religion. After this, Sabra visited him oftener; and as his strength failed, and the world receded, Heaven appeared more glorious. In a few days he sank quietly to rest, as calmly as the sun disappears at evening, leaving his friends to mourn their loss, which was his gain.

CHAPTER XL.

SABRA COMMENCES TEACHING SCHOOL.

Sabra had purchased a comfortable house, and land sufficient for their use, with the money that had been willed to her previous to her second marriage, and was much attached to her new home.

During the second year after her marriage she was alone the most of the time.

After the birth of her daughter, which they named Ordelia, she seemed possessed with great energy. Her husband was a Canadian, but had resided in the States for some years; soon after the birth of her daughter, business called him back to Canada for the season. Immediately after he was gone, Sabra made arrangements to commence the task for which she had been so long preparing. She obtained a nurse for her child, and took two rooms of her house for her scholars. She found many friends willing to patronize and assist her,

She commenced with sixteen scholars, but her number increased rapidly ; she soon had forty-eight; this was all she could accommodate. She found it a delightful task " to teach the young ideas how to shoot." She often enjoyed precious seasons while she bowed daily with her scholars to supplicate the blessings of God to rest upon them, her family and herself. She wrote to her friends, and informed them how she was employed. They wondered how she became qualified to teach a school. Samuel said, " I always told you that Sabra was ambitious, and would take care of herself." Ah ! they little knew how many midnight hours she had spent over her books, or the joy that thrilled through her soul when she reached out her hand to take her certificate, after having passed a strict examination.

After having taught more than two years, at intervals, a clergyman inquired of her, why his children made such rapid progress in learning. Three of his children had attended her school not quite a year ; they had all commenced in A B C, and now they could read any book. She replied, that she could easily tell him ; they attended regularly, and as soon as they could read, he supplied them with books that they could understand. He had a large library, and kept a large supply of books, published by the American Tract Society, which are very entertaining to children. If parents would always supply their children with books that they could understand, they would love to read them, and soon acquire a taste for learning.

Sabra's health became impaired by constant labor, and symptoms of consumption again appeared; she had a cough, and her lungs were affected. Herbert thought she had better visit her friends, and spend the winter; she did so, and visited at Jason's and Samuel's with her mother, the whole season. They all seemed pleased to see her, and she enjoyed her visit very much. They all loved little Ordelia; she was a lovely child. How often, in the still hours of the night, would the sad thought pass through Sabra's mind that she must go back. Alas! who can tell the depth of sorrow that often filled her heart, when she thought that she must leave her dear mother, in her old age, and return, as if an exile. She would not have desired to have shared their luxuries, or to have been surrounded with splendor like theirs. No; she would have been contented with an humble abode, if her companion had been there; and she could have enjoyed their society, for her heart twined tenderly around the whole family still. Samuel often said that he wished she lived near; but she saw nothing flattering, why she could induce her husband to leave his abode, and come there to live. Mrs. Hudson called her son's wives and Sabra her girls; and when they were all together, she would talk of her household property. She had a large quantity of beds and bedding, and rich clothing; she wished them all to share equally; said that they might as well have them divided then, what she did not wish to use; she had a valuable shawl, which she wished to give to

Henrietta, as she was the eldest; she had often told her to take it, but she had not taken it. Marina said there was no use in her giving them away, but let them remain as long as she lived; perhaps she might need them herself. Sabra knew that Samuel and Jason endeavored to make their mother comfortable when she was with them, but her home was at Fred's, and she did not enjoy herself while there ; there was always so much to do ; there was no time to harness a horse for her and she might as well go to church with him as to go where she had always attended, while her husband was living.

When Sabra returned, Samuel's eldest daughter, Eveline, went home with her, and spent the summer. Sabra loved all her nephews and nieces; they were very kind to her, and she liked to have them with her. There seemed but one abiding consolation for her; this she found in the performance of her religious duties, which brought peace and comfort to her mind.

Shortly after Eveline went home, Herbert's friends influenced him to go to Canada; they wished him to move his family there; they gave him great encouragement ; assured him that he would be successful in business. They were very comfortable where they were ; had a large comfortable house of their own. Sabra felt sure to leave their home would be to lose it, but what could she say; it was the home of Herbert's childhood, and his mother lived there ; she knew very well how happy it would cause her to be, to return

to the place of her nativity. Herbert said he
would go and stay a few months, and see what
his prospects were, before he moved his family there.
After this, a friend of Herbert's came to persuade
her to leave her comfortable home. He was a member
of the church, agreeable in his manners, rich and influential; -he held forth many inducements in favor of,
their moving, such as the business man often makes.
He told Sabra that she might be assured of good society,
that she would have the society and friendship of his
family. She knew that this was an inducement, for
their reputation was known as influential. She taught
her school six months after her husband left, having
good success and visited her future home during the
time. She was well pleased with the circle into which
she was introduced; still her heart was pained within
her, to leave her old friends; there were a thousand
ties to bind her there; there was their minister and
his family; the church to which they both belonged; the
dear children who had attended her school; their convenient house; and finally the home which she had toiled
to obtain; all this she left, and went to Canada, as her
future home. She soon found all her early prejudices
destroyed, for she loved the people there, and found
them very kind; she found also, to her sorrow, that
the same spirit influenced the business men there,
in Canada, which existed in other places; simply this,
to keep what they possessed, and to get what they
could; and there are but very few exceptions to this

rule of practice, even among professors of religion; but this is not the Gospel rule, which teaches us to do unto others as we would wish them to do by us. There are many, benevolent men, who profess to possess the religion of the Gospel, and think they follow their Saviour, who give their hundreds of dollars for popular purposes, and take it wrongfully from the poor.

After they had lived in Canada more than a year, they visited Sabra's mother for the last time. Sabra soon saw that her mother was failing fast, and that she was depressed in her mind. She spoke freely to Sabra of her trouble; said that her home was not in the right family, or where it should have been. It was true, she had the privilege of staying with Jason, or Samuel, whenever she chose, yet it was not her home. One subject weighed heavily upon her mind; she had felt it her duty to unite with the church where she always attended worship when her husband was living. Fred had persuaded her to go with him; he told her that there was no use in harnessing a horse for her, when she could hear just as good preaching; that her minister did not visit her. She yielded to his request in this case, as she had in all others. She said if she could enjoy the privilege of conversing with Mrs. Heulet, as she formerly had, it would be a great comfort, but they were watched narrowly; if Mrs. Heulet came there to see her, Marina would always be present, and so glad to see her; if she went to see Mrs. Heulet, Marina would go, too, saying that it was not prudent for her to be left alone. She told Sabra that she was afraid she would be deprived of her reason, by being disappointed in everything; but one thing remained sure ; she had provided for Jason, and for her, in her will, and she hoped that they would attend to it, after her death.   Sabra begged her not to have any trouble on her account; she could take care of herself ; she encouraged her to hope for future happiness beyond this vale of tears.

When they returned, Jason's eldest daughter, Hatty, went home with them.   She was much attached to Sabra, and a mutual friendship always existed between them.   No person surmised that Sabra was not her own dear aunt.   When Sabra's second daughter was born, many exclaimed :   " How much she looks like Hatty !"   and she was named after her, immediately. Hatty was a dear, good girl ; she loved her grandma, and many a long talk would Sabra and Hatty have about her, expressing to each other the fears they had that she would become insane by disappointment. Hatty remained nearly a year, and then returned home, leaving her aunt to mourn her absence.

CHAPTER XL

MRS. HUDSON'S DEATH AND SAMUEL'S VISIT TO CANADA.

Soon after Hatty returned, she wrote to her aunt, informing her that what they had feared was actually the case ; her grandma was deprived of her reason,

and so much deranged that it often became necessary to confine her; she did not know her children;
that Samuel would often try to have her recognize
him as her youngest, or her babe, as she once
called him, but she would sneer at him, saying
that he need not say that to her, for he was not
her child; that she had no children there. Oh, how
bitterly did Sabra mourn for her mother; she could
not see her, neither could she desire to, if she could
not be recognized by her. She remained in this distressing condition for a few months, when death ended
the sufferings of one of the kindest and most indulgent
mothers ever known; an affectionate and loving wife;
a kind and obliging neighbor, a faithful friend, an
humble, devoted Christian. She had but one visible
error; she allowed her children to govern her. This
great mistake caused unhappiness in the whole family
circle.

Grievously did Sabra mourn for the death of her
dear mother; but she was far, far away, and could
not hear the particulars respecting her sickness or
death. Samuel had become rich, and thought he
would travel. The death of his mother had left a
deep impression upon his mind. He thought he would
go to Canada, and see Sabra. He arrived there quite
unexpectedly; Sabra had been thinking of him all the
morning, for she had been making succotash for
dinner; she had often prepared it for him before her
marriage. She was overjoyed to see him; her first

thoughts were, she could hear all about her mother's sickness and death. After dinner, she began to ask him questions about her; but alas! his answer. He said: "Yes; mother is dead, and gone; but I do not wish you to ask me any questions about her, for I do not wish to think of her. She has gone where she is free from trouble." As soon as Sabra could leave the room, she found a place to weep and pray. "Oh," thought she, "and he will not tell me about my best friend; he does not wish to think about his dear mother. If I could have been permitted to have rocked for her the cradle of declining life, she might have ended her days peacefully, with a bright prospect of Heaven."

Samuel liked Herbert; he thought he had good talents for business. After they had returned from church on the Sabbath, Samuel and Herbert were talking of opportunities for making money; men of business will often do this, if they do profess religion. Herbert spoke of a great water privilege, about thirty miles distant, which could be bought cheap; it was surrounded with standing timber which would make good lumber. Samuel said: "That is just the place for you; you can saw the lumber and ship it to our market, and we can make a fortune; let us see Mr. C., (he was their nearest neighbor,) and see what he says?" Mr. C. knew all about it, and had talked about purchasing it himself. They went to Mr. C.; he recommended it highly. It was decided that they would go and see it the next day.   M

As soon as Sabra saw Herbert alone, she told him
not to accept any partnership or help from Samuel ;
he had undertaken to help her once, and that was
all she desired.   If he chose to give them money, she
would accept it thankfully, but she wished not to be
connected in business with him again.   She had never
told Herbert of their ill luck while in business with him,
or of the many sleepless nights she had worked, to pay
the debt they owed him when they closed their business.   She knew that he was rich, in railroad stock
and bank stock; that he could boast of giving one
thousand dollars towards building the church, and
owned two shares in the church organ, besides giving
fifty dollars at a time to the Missionary Society, but
she did not ask his assistance.   Before they started,
in the morning, Sabra informed Samuel, plainly, that
whatever arrangement they might make, she would
never go there to live.   Samuel said ; " Why not ? it
is is just the place to make money."   She said, she
intended to live where her children could attend school :
she valued an education more highly than money ;
that there was no road to that place; that it laid upon
the Rideau Lake; that it was accessible only by boats
or on foot; if he chose to move his family there, she
was willing. He had but two daughters; one married,
and the other old enough to attend a boarding-school ;
her children were young, and she should not go. This
assertion put a damper upon all his calculations; they
went to see it, yet did not purchase it.   He became

acquainted with the family that lived there. The lady
of the house took care to entertain them ; she was
acquainted with Sabra, and said to Samuel, she wished
that he had brought his sister out with him ; that she
esteemed her highly. " Yes," said Samuel, " she is
a very amiable person, well calculated to get along,
brings up her family well ;" but, feeling a little chagrined at the difference in their worldly prospects, he
said, " She is only my adopted sister." This surprised the lady very much ; she inquired if Hatty was
not Sabra's niece. He replied: " She is my niece,
but not Sabra's own niece." She had often remarked,
how much little Hatty looked like her cousin. This
lady merely mentioned it to two or three persons, but
it spread like fire in the prairies, and it became tea-
table talk. Some had it that Mr. Hudson was Sabra's
adopted brother, and others declared it otherwise.
No person mentioned it to Sabra for nearly a year,
when Mrs. Inquisitive thought she would ask Sabra
which of the two persons was the adopted child. Sabra
told her that it was herself. She quietly dropped her
spectacles back upon her nose, and said : " It beats
me ; why, how is it that you have the best education ?
Why didn't you tell me ?" Sabra said that her mother
had often told her not to mention it, for that was her
only dear mamma. Samuel gave up the idea of spe-
culation in the back woods. He was pleased with
Ordelia's appearance and seemed much attached to
her, he thought her an excellent scholar, and wished

her parents to send her to live with him when she was older and he would keep her at school. This pleased Ordelia exceedingly, for she had a great desire to acquire an education. She looked forward with great pleasure to the time when she could go to her uncle's, and go to school.

CHAPTER XLII.

SABRA AGAIN VISITS THE HOME OF HER CHILDHOOD— TAKES ORDELIA TO HER UNCLE'S, EXPECTING TO LEAVE HER—RETURNS, AND FINDS THEIR PROPERTY ALL GONE.

Four years have elapsed. We find Ordelia in her fourteenth year. Sabra had been saving means and preparing Ordelia clothing that she might leave her one or two years to go to school. They had a pleasant journey. Ordelia loved to view the scenery; she · admired all the beauties of nature, and often spoke of the wisdom of God in their creation.

They went to Jason's first. There she heard the particulars of her mother's sickness and death; it was even more painful than she had imagined. They spoke of her will. She had told them of it. There had been nothing said concerning it since her death. Fred had complained that his task had been greater than any other member of the family. They concluded that Fred might have all he could get, and they would not look for the will. Marina had taken the shawl, and wore it first to their mother's funeral; she never said anything to Henrietta. When Marina put the shawl over her shoulders, the day of the funeral, Willie's wife said : "I thought grandma gave that shawl to aunt Henrietta." Jason said he would like to know what they would give Sabra; he supposed she would receive her portion while at Fred's. She replied, that she would inform them after her return what they gave her.

They next went to Samuel's. He had built an elegant house, and was surrounded with luxuries of every kind. They enjoyed their visit exceedingly. Asenath was the same kind sister that she had been in former years.

Samuel's youngest daughter Ordelia was preparing to be married. Sabra thought that she had taken her Ordelia there in just the right time, for she would be company for her aunt; but she would wait and see if they invited her to stay before she mentioned that she had brought her there for that purpose. One day Ordelia was with her aunt Sabra, while she was at her trunk. She espied some winter clothing, and exclaimed, " What is that, aunt ? Did you expect to require *that* in the summer ?" She replied that she did not know, but she should leave her cousin somewhere among her friends to go to school. They dropped the conversation for that time. A few days after, Samuel broached the subject. Said he : " I should like very well to have Ordelia stop with us, and go to school ; but I do not

think our school is very good; our French teacher is
not as well qualified as he should be. The music teacher
is not good either. Ordelia has been giving lessons to
our minister's daughter and two or three others; it has
been too much for her. To be sure she is going to
board out the first year, and will not have much to do,
but I do not want she should bother her brains teaching
music." Said he, "I suppose Ordelia wishes to study
French, and music, and all the extra branches." Sabra
replied that was what she wished, for she would acquire
a good common education at home; "it has cost me a
large sum of money to educate my daughter." Said
Samuel, "I feel poor, and my wife has poor health; it
would be a great responsibility on her to have Ordelia
remain." There was nothing more said about Ordelia
staying. She was not as cheerful after this, and did not
feel well, and was very glad to go home. Samuel's
eldest daughter, Eveline, was married. They visited
her, and then went to Fred's. Samuel and his wife
and daughter went with them. Sabra thought them
very kind; for she thought it would be very lonesome
there without her mother. They all appeared very
cheerful and happy; but Sabra's heart was full of sorrow; it was there her dear mother had suffered and died.
She stole away, and walked a mile and a half to her
mother's grave; there the tears could flow unrestrained.
When she returned, she felt more reconciled. Marina
was very pious; they could hear her voice, up stairs,
engaged in secret prayer, nearly as loud as when the

prophets of Baal called upon their God. Sabra wondered if she was sincere. They stayed two nights; they were sleepless ones to her. The home of her childhood, where she had spent her happiest hours; the peach tree, which had grown from the peach she had planted with her own hand when young, seemed to wave its heavy branches mournfully. There was the tree under which she had made her little playhouse : but now the noise created by the wind among its branches seemed to howl a requiem for the dead. Sabra did not covet their possessions; she looked forward to a glorious home, where she would meet her parents with joy; she loved to think of them; she had no remorse of conscience; even her dreams of them were delightful.

A short time before they left, Sabra was in the hall arranging her trunk. Marina hastened to her, bringing two cups and saucers. Said she to Sabra, " I thought you would like these; you have often drunk tea from them with mother. They are cracked, but I thought you would like them if they were old." Sabra took them kindly, her eyes filled with tears, while Marina tripped off, singing merrily. She packed them carefully away in her trunk, that they might not be broken ; it was all she had given her, and she would keep them choicely. Marina returned to her, singing as usual, saying, " I have brought you this silver-plate it was on mother's coffin; it is of no use to us. I will give this to you ; perhaps you will like to keep it; we thought there was no use to have it buried." Sabra took it thankfully, but she thought it strange that they removed it from the coffin. " Ah !" thought Sabra, " how can she speak so unfeelingly of one of the best of mothers." Her gifts reminded her of Marina's visit at her brother Jason's. She had been out shopping, and she purchased a paper of lozenges, for which she paid three pence ; she carried them to the house, and this Christian philanthropist gave them all to her niece, saying, " It is more blessed to give than to receive;" but before she went away, she asked her niece for a few of them to carry to her mother Bronson, for she was going to visit her before she returned.

They visited Mrs. Heulet's family, and found them the same devoted Christians that they were in Sabra's youthful days.

Mrs. Heulet had a daughter married, and living in O——, New York. When Sabra and Ordelia returned, Mrs. H. accompanied them on a visit to her daughter.

Mrs. Heulet was not accustomed to travelling on the boats ; she thought them dangerous, but Sabra thought it would be a change, and give her rest to take the boat at Burlington. She consented, and went on board. Sabra left them in the beautiful cabin, and went to see to the baggage, &c. The boat had already started. The lake was very calm, there was scarcely any motion. She went into the cabin, and they were admiring the beauty of the furniture and the richness of the tapestry.

After about an hour, Mrs. H. enquired how long they were to be detained in B——. She was surprised to find that they were half way across the lake. She gave up the idea of being sick, and went on deck to view the beauties of the scenery. They enjoyed their trip exceedingly.

As Sabra journeyed toward her humble home, her mind was occupied with various subjects. Many of the ties which bound her so strongly to her native home were sundered ; she thought if she only arrived at home safely, and was permitted again to embrace her children —little Herbert, he was the youngest, a dear little boy —if she could find them all in the enjoyment of health, she should be willing to toil for them, and never be dis contented. She had often read, over and over, the let- ters on Palestine, in the Olive Branch, and desired to know who wrote them ; she had been informed that it was a dear and near relative of her own, and she was anxious to get home and find the papers, and read them again, for she always kept these papers laid by, after they were read ; it proved to her a weekly epistle· to cheer her lonely hours.

Sabra found her family all well, and her happiness seemed increased by thinking they were all together. The joy of this meeting had not subsided before she had to realize another sad disappointment. She found that her husband had been unsuccessful in his business ; and, like many others, he too had become penniless, and not only so, but was also involved. Many

in this section remember the year 1857 with sorrow.
They are still held by the powerful grip of the creditor,
and thereby unable to pay their debts, or support
their families. It was then that Sabra began to think
of the future prospects of her children. She wished
that Ordelia had stayed with her uncle. She thought
how unkind it was in him, after urging them to send
her there, and after they had taken her there and been
to so much trouble, that he should not have her remain.

But, was Sabra discouraged? No ! She who had
known what poverty was before, knew that it would
do no good to fret. Said she to her husband, " I will
not sink, without an effort to keep my head above the
water. I can teach school again ; and I think I could
write a book." Said he " You could not get it printed
if you had it written." This answer damped her
ambition, but she kept silent, and applied herself to her
manuscript every leisure hour ; always asking God's
assisting grace that she might be directed in writing
that which would have a moral and religious influence
on the minds of those who might favor her with their
patronage. She thought by this effort she might assist
her family, and educate her children.

CHAPTER XLIII.

SAMUEL HEARS OF THEIR MISFORTUNE, AND WRITES
HERBERT A LETTER.—THE DEATH OF EVELINE.

The following is an extract from the letter :—" I
am sorry to hear that you have not succeeded in your

business, as you expected : but it is only one of the disappointments that flesh is heir to. I also thought my mountain stood strong, in respect to this world, when I was at your place, but a great share of it has fled. I have lost thousands of dollars, and I sometimes get low-spirited; but we have much to be thankful for yet. Our children are spared. We would not lose one of them for all worldly prosperity."

"Ah!" said Sabra, " what a blessed privilege would it be to the professor of religion, if the Bible taught not the doctrine of restitution!" but, alas! for multitudes it is found in Holy Writ in many places. The next letter they received contained intelligence of the death of Eveline. Sabra could sympathize with them. She had buried a daughter, and time had not erased it from her memory.

CHAPTER XLIV.

MRS. C—— KINDLY OFFERS ORDELIA A HOME IN THEIR FAMILY WHERE SHE HAD THE PRIVILEGE OF ACQUIRING AN EDUCATION.—SABRA TEACHES SCHOOL —FINISHES HER MANUSCRIPT, AND SUCCEEDS IN GETTING IT PRINTED.

Ordelia's greatest trouble was that she could not acquire a thorough education. She could bear the reproaches of the world with others, if she could be qualified for teaching.

Providence seemed to smile upon her. Mrs.C——,

of O——, (Mrs. Heulet's daughter) kindly invited her to accept a home with her, and go to the institute. There she could have every privilege she desired.

Sabra commenced teaching school in L——, C. W., and succeeded in getting as many scholars as she could accommodate.

When she had leisure, she would write in her manuscript. When she had it completed, she submitted it to five or six gentlemen, who were competent judges, for examination. These gentlemen recommended it to the public.

The next question was : how could she get it published ? She had some property in the States ; but how to make it apply, she could not tell, but a kind Providence opened the way. Friends kindly offered to assist her.

The publishers were generous in their terms of payment ; and in 1858 her book was ready for sale. Her first edition was five thousand. "Five thousand !" says one of Sabra's neighbors ; " is the woman crazy ? surely she can never expect to sell them all ; and certainly she can never pay for them."

Sabra closed her school and commenced the task herself. She was not easily discouraged. She canvassed many of the towns in St. Lawrence County, and found a ready sale. She chose to canvass in Canada, for this was now her home. She found the people kind and benevolent, and willing to patronize her. She also received many recommendations through the press. The greatest trial she experienced while selling the book, was her absence from her family; she would so arrange her task, that she would only be away six or eight weeks at a time. In this way she could assist her family and keep her children at school.

CHAPTER XLV.

SABRA'S LETTER TO HER DAUGHTER.

This letter was given to Ordelia by her mother, as advice to her when she left home to attend school. It was the closing chapter in the first edition. It may be the language of many a pious mother:

" My Dear Ordelia,—My eldest daughter, you are about to leave your parental home, that you may more effectually climb the hill of Science; you may continually be ascending, but you cannot reach the top. No person ever obtained the summit of knowledge. We only commence in this world what eternity may finish. It has always been our aim to have you acquire an education; yet I feel more anxious for your moral and religious culture. No toil has been spared by your mother, to teach you, in childhood, the duty you owe to your Maker and Preserver, and to your fellow beings. Be kind and affable to all; be particularly respectful to the aged and infirm, treat them as your superiors; always choose the virtuous and the good for your associates; never countenance vice. Never circulate an evil report; remember, if you repeat a falsehood, you give credit to the same. Always be willing to help build up the character of the poor and virtuous. If you acquire an education, and make a right use of it, you will treat all with respect. Should you gain the estimation of those who are wealthy, never, on this account, slight an old friend, if they are poor. I have seen young ladies (I should have said girls) return home from boarding-school, who had only been there three months; their associates have counted the day before their arrival and longed to greet them; but judge their disappointment, when they met, they could not be recognized. Think not that such conduct is commendable; they only make themselves a subject of ridicule. If you are slighted, never notice it. A trifling slight often becomes an injury by pondering on it. You have attended a Sabbath-school, from your childhood; endeavour to profit by the instructions you have there received. You have recited a large portion of the Holy Scriptures; if possible, read a chapter every day.

> 'Tis God's own word, which he has given,
> To teach your soul the way to Heaven.

Remember that they may all be summed up, in a few verses: 'Thou shall love the Lord, thy God, with all thy heart, with all thy soul, and with all thy mind; and thou shalt love thy neighbour as thyself. Therefore, all things that ye would that men should do to you, do ye even so to them.' And the conclusion of the whole is this: 'Fear God, and keep His com-

mandments;' attend church regularly, and listen
attentively to the public administration of God's word.
Seek to obtain the saving, regenerating grace of God.
Never let the imperfections of professors of religion
hinder you from becoming a Christian. The very
fact that you know that they are wrong, may rise
up to condemn you at the last day, for having known
your Heavenly Father's will, and having neglected to
perform it. It is to be feared that many will approach
so near the track which leads to glory, that the car of
salvation will pass over them, and literally grind them
to powder. Life is a mixture of joy and sorrow,
smiles and tears, disappointments, crosses, bereave-
ments, grief and pain, and finally death ; but remember
that you were created for a high and noble purpose.
God has provided a higher, holier, and happier home
for us, if we are prepared by his pardoning mercy
and sanctifying grace. He has invited us to mingle
with the bright intelligences of saints and angels,
who continually surround the throne: and the capaci-
ties of your soul, for enjoyment, will continue to enlarge,
while you contemplate His wonderful works, His
glorious attributes, His infinite perfections. And when
you drop this body of clay, your nobler faculties will
be illumined with the blazing lustre of glory, and your
soul filled with the fulness of God : you will there find
flowers that never fade, and fruit that never decays.
Remember, you were a peculiar blessing to me in the
time of affliction, sent to claim the affection once

bestowed upon those whom God took to himself. The wounded heart of your mother had scarcely time to heal, ere it would be called to break forth with sorrow, by the removal of one dear relative after another. The year previous to your birth, I was called to part with my only beloved child. The vacancy which her death caused, was never filled until I received you, as it were, in her place. I loved you tenderly, and have endeavoured to guard you from temptation. Being deprived of wealth, I have toiled to bring you up respectably, and give you an education. Thus far you have rewarded me, by the progress you have made, by your kindness and fidelity. I desire that you may continue to improve your time faithfully in the future. There is one request that I wish to make of you: that you would always continue to have a watchful care over your little brother and sister, they are much younger than yourself, and may not enjoy a mother's protection as long as you have. Try to guard them as you have been. Show them the kindness you have received: and try, if possible, to help them to acquire an education. Take this letter with you to your school: keep it laid by safely, and occasionally read it, remembering that it is accompanied by the prayer of your

"AFFECTIONATE MOTHER."

CHAPTER XLVI.

JASON SENDS TO SABRA FOR ONE OF HER BOOKS—
HIS OPINION OF IT—HE VISITS HER—HIS DEATH.

Jason heard of Sabra's book, and sent to her for one.
After obtaining a promise from him that he would give
her his opinion of it, she sent him one. We will give
his answer in his own words :

" DEAR SISTER.—I like your book for many reasons.
It brings vividly to my mind the scenes of my childhood ; it causes me to laugh and to weep. I only wish
that my dear wife Henrietta had lived to have read it.
I do not know that it contains an untrue sentence. I
wish every member of our family had one to read.

" This is my humble opinion. You may come and
make my house your home, and sell it here, if you wish.
It would sell well in this section.

" Yours affectionately,
" J. H."

Sabra was rejoiced to read this letter, for she feared
he might be displeased. She always had a great
desire that he should visit her. In July, 1860, while
Ordelia was at home spending vacation, he came,
accompanied by his daughter Sabra. They were all
rejoiced to see them. They visited some of the
romantic places in Canada together, such as Marble
Rock and its surrounding lakes. They visited Herbert's
mother and brother. Jason admired the fields of

N

wheat which grew luxuriantly on either side of the
road.   He was not accustomed to see this kind of
grain growing in old Massachusetts.   He amused
himself by hunting, fishing, shooting at target, and
picking berries, which grew abundantly that season.
He liked the people of Canada ; thought he would
like to live there ; said he would go home and arrange
his business, and perhaps he would come there to
reside.   He had buried his wife and felt very lonely
at home.   They stayed a month : visited Mrs. C. and
Mrs. Judson's family, and returned home, when
Ordelia went back to school.

The next letter Sabra received from them contained
the sad intelligence of her dear brother's death.   This
was quite unexpected, for his health seem'd to improve
while he stayed with them ; and they had anticipated
much pleasure in having him come there to live.

CHAPTER XLVII.

ORDELIA RETURNS HOME FROM SCHOOL—ACQUIRES A
FIRST-CLASS CERTIFICATE—COMMENCES TEACHING
AND IS SUCCESSFUL—HER PLANS FOR FUTURE USE-
FULNESS—HER DEATH.

Ordelia returned home, having acquired a thorough
education.   She was the picture of health, the joy and
hope of her parents.   At the sitting of the Board of
Education in F——, C. W., she received a first-class
certificate.   Her capacity for teaching was equal to her

education. Her hopes were brilliant. She obtained a school near home, and gave good satisfaction. At the close of the first term she engaged for the ensuing year. Said she : "Mother, you have toiled hard to assist me to get an education ; now, I can help you, and my sister, and brother; I can give Minnie lessons in French, and can assist Herbert in Mathematics, and *perhaps* we can relieve father of his embarrassments, if you are as successful as you have been."

But, alas! how soon were all their earthly hopes blasted ! Incessant study and the anxiety for the progress of her scholars brought on disease which terminated suddenly in inflammation of the brain : and the 7th of Sept., 1861, these fond parents were called to part with their dear beloved daughter ; and these children, bereft of their dear sister, to whom they had often looked for favors and for counsel.

She had been the sunlight of that family for nearly twenty years, apparently healthy and qualified for usefulness, beloved by all who knew her. How could they give her up! Nothing but the grace of God could sustain them under this afflicting dispensation of providence.

After the solemnities of the funeral were over, how lonely was their home ! How could Sabra leave them to finish the sale of her books. The time for the last payment had passed. The publishers had not even reminded her of it. They had always been very kind : but Sabra felt her responsibility ; and with her heart burdened with sorrow, she went to Montreal. She had canvassed there before. It was not like going to a strange place ; she found the people hospitable and kind and willing to patronize her. She sold over four hundred books in that city. This more than completed the payment for her book, and she could remain at home during the winter. But, oh ! how lonely was her home ; how often was she reminded of that dear daughter !

In the summer of 1862, Sabra went to St. Catherines, to Hamilton, and the villages near there, and finished the sale of the first edition. The success and the encouragement which she has had from that time to the present, has induced her to get this fourth edition.

No person can travel in Canada, without admiring the kindness and hospitality of the people. It has been this that has cheered Sabra onward in her laborious task. She still hopes, by selling this book, to bring up her children decently, and qualify them for usefulness.

With the sincere thanks of the authoress to those who have patronized her, and to the public generally, we will close this Narrative.

THE END.